Colonel Weston's Wedding

Regency Novella

Lynda Dunwell

Copyright © 2016 Lynda Dunwell

ISBN-13:978-1-910712-10-8

Publisher's note:
This book is a work of fiction. Name, characters,
places and incidents either are the product of the
author's imagination or are used fictitiously.

Cover Design:
Selfpubbookcovers.com/ineedabookcover

CHAPTER ONE

London 1818

Colonel Richard Weston picked up two cards. A potential winning hand? Poker-faced he raised the stakes and waited for the two remaining gentlemen in the round to respond.

The next player, Sydney Moreton, held his cards close to his chest. "Dashed high stakes Weston, or does your mother give you leave to gamble away the fruits of an estate which ain't legally hers?"

"If you refer to Moreton Arnscote, take that back sir," Richard demanded. "No gentleman discusses a respectable lady at the gaming table. Take it back or I'll see you at first light down the barrel of a pistol."

Heads turned as the prospect of a duel flashed around the gaming room of the fashionable St. James' club.

"Tut, tut, can't you see the pun? Meant to jest of course but ain't it rum? I'm gambling to win a mite of what's my own. Ironic, I'd say, ironic. Fortunate I ain't so dull of humour I can't see the pun of it. Although, if it ain't deuced awkward." He glanced around the card room of the club. "I appeal to you gentlemen, what's a fellow to do? Got good claim on title and inheritance, yet barred from my birthright by my aunt who insists her brother-in-law lives." He paused to mop his brow with his silk handkerchief. "And what of my uncle, the elusive Captain Henry Moreton? The world ain't seen hide nor hair of the old sea dog since Trafalgar!"

Richard glared at Sydney but refused to rise to his bait." As the widow of the late Sir William, my mother, Lady Moreton, has every right to remain at Moreton Arnscote until ownership has been decided by Chancery. Although you claimed both title and estate on the very day my step-father died you will have to be more patient. If Captain Henry Moreton lives, he is the rightful heir."

Richard had disliked his step-cousin from boyhood and assumed the feeling was mutual. However, he knew Sydney well enough to know there was no risk in challenging him. The man would not dare face him alone.

"Come on coz, no bad feeling intended," Sydney said, "perhaps I was little hasty when my dear uncle passed on, poor fellow, was never the same after Charles fell. Could never understand how a man allowed his only son to march to the sound of the drum."

Richard seethed, inwardly fighting to control

his anger. Sydney always was a manipulating cad who knew how to goad an opponent. But that knowledge didn't release him from the weight of guilt he carried over his half-brother's demise at Waterloo. He eyed Sydney intently, determined to let the fellow wriggle on the hook as befitted the worm he was. "Retract or face me tomorrow at dawn."

Sydney's plump face turned puce. "My apologies Weston, I meant the lady no ill, but the whole world knows your estate ain't large and as gentlemen we can't live on nought, can we? I'd wager she has had to come to your rescue when the tables ran against you, eh?"

"Do not insult me further Moreton, or I will have you blackballed from this club."

"Now, now, there's no need to go that far, what's a slight disagreement between family members, eh? You're the same as the rest of us young bucks keen to wed money if you can't inherit it, eh? But fortune shines upon the righteous, 'tis said. I won't have to wait much longer for my inheritance, then not a drawing room in England will be closed to me. Title and estate rightfully mine, mark my words."

Annoyed by his opponent's fanciful claims, Richard wished he hadn't agreed to the obnoxious fellow sitting at their table, or that they were connected, albeit only by marriage.

Attempting to silence him he asked, "Are you staying in this round?"

"Of course I am." Sydney turned to the next player. "My man of affairs has tracked down a Captain Henry Moreton in Devonshire. If he is my uncle, then sadly the fellow's recently gone to his Maker, so 'though my claim on the title was a little premature, fancy I'll get the lot in the end. Care to take my I.O.U on the strength of it Thompson?"

"That depends of Colonel Weston position," the gentleman replied.

Sydney huffed and turned back to Richard. "Perhaps we'll see how eviction suits the dowager, besides I have a fancy to trim Mrs. Peacock's feathers by stripping her of the Moreton sapphires. There are more tender necks I'd like to see those jewels grace."

In no mood to fence verbally with Sydney's vile tongue any longer Richard replied, "I will not accept your I.O.U sir, now are you in or out?"

Sydney's lips thinned and his dark eyes flashed. Scowling he cast his cards on the table, rose and quit the card room.

Richard looked across the table at his final opponent. "How are you playing sir?"

Mr. Thompson spread his cards on the table. "Moreton's hand would have beaten me."

Richard glanced at the upturned cards and nodded. "But not my four kings." He placed his hand on the table. "Care for another round, gentlemen?"

The rest of the players agreed which pleased Richard who believed luck had finally begun to run with him. However, as he shuffled the pack, a note was delivered. He took it from the silver salver, recognised his step-father's seal and knew it was from his mother. He broke the seal and read the contents. Lady Moreton demanded his presence urgently at Moreton Arnscote. *It has come!* She had scrawled in her extravagant hand. *My destruction! I shall be cast out, homeless, unless you assist me! If you have any compassion for your distraught mother, return at once. Not a moment must be lost!*

Caroline Moreton felt the warmth of the afternoon sun on her face as she sat by the cottage window and picked up the letter she had received earlier. She read it again. Time had not improved neither its tone nor the contents. In a neat hand the writer acknowledged Captain Henry Moreton's communication and informed her in the same sentence of Sir William Moreton's death two years before. And as a consequence of her claim to being a *near* relative, a claim which Caroline had certainly never made, she was summoned forthwith to Moreton Arnscote.

My representative will call upon you during the morning of the 17th instant this month, April, and provide escort to Staffordshire. The letter was signed in a flamboyant second hand Margaret Moreton.

On first receipt Caroline nearly cast it into the fire, except she had no fire in the hearth. She had only sent her father's letter because it had been his final wish. Without breaking his seal, she had added a note confirming the date of his death on the outside.

Ignorant of the extent of her father's debt until his death, all her possessions had been sold to meet the demands made upon her in her father's name. The cottage on the North Devonshire coast, the only home she had known, was to be taken at the end of the month because she could not repay the loan which had been secured against it. Her situation appeared desperate. In a few short weeks her life had changed from one of contentment as the daughter of a retired navy captain to that of a pauper.

She had sought work, but few houses would take her on as a servant, younger lower-class girls were preferred who could be trained to their exact requirements. At eighteen, she was too young for a housekeeper but a position as a governess might suit. However, without connections a post was proving hard to secure. At least she had a good character reference from Mr. Hawkins, the local vicar, who had baptised her eighteen years ago. She re-read the letter. Perhaps the summons to Moreton Arnscote, although initially unwelcoming, might secure her future after all?

Early on the morning of the 17th a carriage of some consequence and bearing a family crest halted outside the cottage. Expecting the Moreton representative, Caroline watched a tall broad-shouldered man descend and stride purposefully towards the front door. Upon hearing the firm knock she descended the stairs and opened the door. The man framed in the doorway was not the type of representative she had imagined.

"Good morning, I am seeking Miss Moreton, I understand she resides within," he said. His lively grey eyes locked with hers. "I have not had the pleasure of Miss Moreton's acquaintance, a matter I hope will soon be amended. Please inform Miss Moreton that Colonel Richard Weston is waiting upon her." He removed his hat and revealed shoulder length light brown hair sun bleached at the extremities.

Taken slightly aback, Caroline didn't like being taken as a servant. However, how many ladies answered the front door? Wouldn't he assume, dressed as she was in a simple grey wool gown that she was in service to Miss Moreton? He spoke like a gentleman and his air was that of politeness. But what of the man? She decided he was about thirty as she looked up at him. However, it was the superior cut of his coat that made him stand out from other gentlemen she had seen. Perhaps the style of his collar and cravat were the height of fashion, yet she had no yardstick with which to compare them. Was his strong face with the interesting steel grey eyes that of a popinjay? No, those features couldn't possibly belong to one who valued the tie of his cravat knot above everything else, however, the elegant man before her was every inch the gentleman. He had a confident air which exuded authority.

"Colonel Weston, perhaps you would care to step inside?" She held the door open for him.

As he crossed the threshold and entered the room she noted a slight hesitancy in his step. Was it the bareness of the cottage? However, he made no mention of it.

She thought she caught an expression of relief on his handsome face, but he quickly concealed it. It would not be gentlemanly, she convinced herself, if he made his true feelings known. However, a large knot began to tie itself in her stomach. Embarrassment? Fear of the unknown? Whatever it was she tried to shrug off the unfamiliar feeling but realised it was nervous anticipation. Colonel Weston was already disturbing her inner calm, hence he would not be the easiest of travelling companions.

"Thank you for coming so promptly Colonel Weston. We have not been formally introduced but I am Caroline Moreton." She dropped a demure bob and lowered her eyes from his. When she looked at him again, she thought she detected a slight expression of surprise.

"My most humble apologies, Miss Moreton for confusing you with a member of your household."

"My baggage is over there." She pointed an unsteady hand towards a battered sea chest that had once been her father's. It clearly bore his initials H.M and a worn crest.

Richard raised his eyebrows. "And your maid?" His eyes swept the small bare room.

"I have no maid."

"Then given the circumstances, the sooner we reach Moreton Arnscote the better. Do you agree?" And without waiting for her reply, he bent down, picked up the chest and made for the door.

Caroline followed him outside and closed the cottage door behind her. She didn't want to look back. She watched the driver and a young groom secure the sea chest to the back of the carriage.

"Please, Miss Moreton, let me assist you," Colonel Weston said and offered her his arm.

She took it and felt the firm grip of his hand at her elbow as he helped her step up into the carriage. It rocked under his powerful frame as he climbed inside and sat opposite her.

So, was this how they were to travel for the next few days? She had no idea how long it would take to journey to Staffordshire, however, she had come this far and if there was the slightest possibility of her aunt's assistance in securing her a position, then a few days travelling with a handsome gentleman seemed at small price to pay.

But she blushed at their close proximity. *He is a stranger* she had to remind herself and fought to control her senses by settling as far back on the padded leather seat as she possibly could. Her back pressed against the carriage seat, she became acutely aware of her pounding heart, pounding so loudly, she was convinced he could hear every thud and would ask her to explain herself.

They set off, taking the coast road and although it was tempting, Caroline did not look out of the window. She had no desire to see her happy childhood home fading into the distance as the carriage took her away. But neither did she want to look at the steely grey eyed man sitting opposite. There was something about him but she could not put her finger on it. The carriage rounded a sharp bend and she grabbed one of the swabs to steady herself. He leaned foward as a shaft of sun struck his hair and it gleamed like dark gold.

"Are you all right?" he asked.

"Yes," she replied, let go of the swab and focused on clasping her gloved hands together on her lap. Perhaps she should have said more, but what could she say? *Your presence disturbs me, I feel restless and irritable sitting opposite you , or your cool aloof manner is irksome.* She didn't know and in her situation decided her best course of action was to keep her own counsel. And so their journey continued in silence.

After a few miles, "I hope I haven't frightened you, Miss Moreton," he drawled with an edge of mockery in his tone, "but are there no inquiries concerning the Moreton family you wish to make of me? Be assured Lady Moreton has given me authority to speak on the matter."

Of course she was curious about the Moretons, but she had no intention of taking him into her confidence and to her annoyance found herself blushing again. "I know nothing of the Moretons so I wouldn't know where to begin." That wasn't strictly true, she admitted silently but his reference to her recent correspondent as Lady Moreton surprised her. She had never imagined her family were related to titled gentry. Of course, she knew her father had written to Sir William Moreton but she had not imagined any close connection. Her father had spoken little of his family life. When she had asked him all his stories were about the sea and his long service in His Majesty's Britannic navy and especially his account of Trafalgar which she knew so well she could relate it by heart. She sent his letter because it had been his dying wish to do so. And she had to confess she had been sorely tempted to open it. If it had been a last desperate effort to contact his family to plead with them to look after her, she did not want to read his begging words. He had been a proud man and she wanted to hold that memory of him.

Glancing across at her companion she decided to plead ignorance of the Moretons. She knew nothing of him or his connection to the family he was representing. "I am sure whatever the Moretons wish to reveal about their family history will be made known to me upon my arrival," she said attempting to use her most confident voice. Whether he believed her or not, she couldn't tell.

He brushed his clean-shaven jaw with his hand. "Miss Moreton, I am intrigued. Could you possibly be one of those rare females who exist in this world without fuelling her curiosity on gossip?"

Caroline couldn't decide whether he was paying her a compliment or mocking her. Assuming it was more likely to be the latter, she tried to work out a way to counter him. But he appeared in control, the essence of a gentleman, and she felt so unworldly. Besides she did not want to dull her chances of securing a recommendation from Lady Moreton regarding the governess situation she sought.

"When we change horses I will attempt to hire a maidservant for you, Miss Moreton," he said.

Fearing she would have to pay the girl's wages, she looked up and met his grey eyes squarely. "I do not consider that necessary. I am perfectly capable of managing alone."

A wide almost condescending expression spread across his face. "I am sure you are, however, it would not be proper for us to travel together without a female companion. I am a bachelor, Miss Moreton and have my reputation to protect."

She knew he was teasing her, what reputation had a gentleman to consider? Perhaps he feared she might declare he had compromised her and demand he do the honourable thing and marry her.

But with no close male relative to put her case, he could easily dismiss her claims as he would those made by a servant. No, it was time for truth. She took a deep breath and said, "Please do not hire a maid on my behalf for I have no money to pay her."

"All expenses will be met by the Moreton estate," he said. "I shall hire the maid whether you agree or not. Proprietary demands it and my own peace of mind requires it."

"So be it," she said. "We shall soon be at the Golden Eagle. Mr. Glynn, the landlord and his wife are known to me. I am sure one of their maids would willingly oblige, if you will guarantee her return."

Richard tried to relax in the carriage. He did not like travelling backwards and regarded carriage riding a necessity to be endured. As a retired cavalry officer he preferred horseback and had every intention of hiring a mount at their first stop. Today he regretted he'd not brought a couple of his own horses down to Devonshire. He had a fine stable and had built his stud steadily since returning home. However, in the close confines of the carriage he decided to use the time as usefully as possible by observing Miss Moreton.

She surprised him. On first acquaintance she appeared rather meek, however, the moment he caught the flash of her lovely green eyes he realised her reticence may only be temporary. She had lost her father a month before and judging by the bareness of her cottage home, she had also lost her main support. But if lack of funds was her problem, why wasn't she more curious about the estate whose family name she shared? Had her father told her nought of his early life? There was undoubtedly a significant conundrum to boot and there was nothing he enjoyed more in a dull moment – a puzzle to solve.

He looked at her again. She was attractive but not pretty, with a few blonde curls escaping from under the plain grey bonnet she wore. The sort of female that would pass as having a tolerable countenance – yes, that's how he would describe her. But he liked his women to have more spirit than she had currently shown. But it was early days. He hoped so. Perhaps she was a poor traveller? He noted that she had taken the forward facing seat without question, but in the few miles they had covered, not once had she glanced through the window or made an attempt to look back at her home. If she was feeling a little queasy, she didn't show it, as for her true nature that might be revealed in greater measure once his mother had taken her safely under her wing. The thought consoled him for a short while. As long as Sydney didn't get hold of her.

The possible inevitability of Sydney getting everything, title, estate and the Moreton sapphires put a bitter taste in his mouth. He took another long look at the girl, she could be no more than eighteen or nineteen years old, easy on the eye and didn't talk incessantly – indeed she had some admirable qualities. But what special attributes did anyone, man or woman need when they had ten thousand a year?

If his mother decided to give her a London Season, she would have her pick of the young bucks and probably secure a title in a matter of weeks. How the fortune-hunters would gather to flatter a lady of substance. Then what would be the girl's fate?

Would she fall in love with one of those worthless fellows who hung on the coat-tails and skirts of richer members of the ton or Heaven forbid, be persuaded to elope. Then what would happen to his mother?

Surely she would be evicted from Arnscote and no doubt settle at Weston Grange. Such a situation would prove intolerable to the most easy temper or affectionate heart. He toyed with the idea of building a dowager house at the Grange and installing his mother in it, but that plan involved persuading her to move there. Somehow he had to fix the young lady before she was let loose in London society. His task was simple. All he needed to do was convince Miss Caroline Moreton, the chief beneficiary of the Moreton estate, of the great honour of becoming Mrs. Weston.

CHAPTER TWO

Caroline glanced out of the carriage and caught a fleeting glimpse of chimneys and turrets. A few moments later the carriage swung into a wide drive and Moreton Arnscote came into full view.

The fine styled hall appeared to be one building, but as the carriage drew closer she noticed a stable block on her right joined to the main house by battlement walls and a turreted gateway.

Tall chimneys rose from the three storey main building which was constructed of sandstone, and two turreted towers stood proud of the main entrance. Under a blue sky, in brilliant sunshine, Moreton Arnscote looked very grand. Caroline drew in breath sharply, what could the Moretons possibly want with her?

Colonel Weston held out his hand to help her down from the carriage. When he hired a maidservant at the Golden Eagle, he had also hired two horses and exchanged them along route when they took on a new team, so he hadn't shared the carriage with her since their first day together. She reached out and placed her hand on his forearm but wasn't prepared for the effect his smile had upon her as her pulse began to race.

"Thank you," she managed to utter and gazed up at the hall rather than face his steel grey inquisition.

"Please allow me to escort you inside." Almost as if he had commanded it, the doors opened and two footmen stood at the entrance.

"Good day Colonel, I trust you had a pleasant journey," a more senior servant asked, whom Caroline thought must be the butler.

"Tolerable," the colonel nodded as he removed his hat and cloak. "Is Lady Moreton at home, Harris?"

"Indeed sir, your arrival has already been observed. Welcome to Moreton Arnscote Miss Moreton. Her ladyship will receive you in the drawing room, if you will kindly come this way?"

She was too surprised to do more than nod, the butler knew her name, she was expected, but the sort of reception she was receiving was more cordial than she had anticipated. However, she followed him obediently. He opened the double doors and stepping to one side announced, "Miss Moreton and Colonel Weston."

"Caroline, I am delighted to have you with us." Lady Moreton held out her hand in a welcoming gesture. "I do hope Richard hasn't been too beastly and frightened you off. He can be quite overpowering at times." She gave him a knowing glance which Caroline thought was almost a silent rebuke. He replied with a mocking grin which convinced her there was some connection between them, but what?

Undoubtedly, Lady Moreton had been a

renowned beauty in her youthful years, Caroline decided, for although in her fifties, her ladyship retained a striking quality which in some women is timeless.

"Come, my dear, I'll show you to your room," Lady Moreton said and took Caroline's arm as if they were old acquaintances reunited.

The slight pressure of Lady Moreton's guiding hand on her arm as they ascended the wide oak staircase only fuelled Caroline's curiosity. How were they connected and what had her father asked Lady Moreton to do? A footman opened the door and she followed Lady Moreton inside.

As she crossed the threshold she took a quick breath of utter astonishment. The gallery along which they had proceeded was dark and heavily panelled, but the interior of this room was quite different. Cream silks blending with ivory damask made it light and airy, whilst the delicate peach shade of the walls added gentle warmth. "It's delightful," she said her eyes scarce able to believe what she saw.

"I'm so pleased you find it to your liking. I want you to feel comfortable at Arnscote," Lady Moreton smiled.

Caroline glanced around the lovely bed chamber. "How could one not feel as ease in such luxurious surroundings?" she said but inwardly it was all too much to take in at once. Who was Lady Moreton and why had she, Caroline Moreton, been brought here? She looked at her ladyship with hope that some of the mystery would soon be unravelled. But an odd feeling started to grow inside her. She didn't know why but the elegant lady before her seemed unlikely to impart readily the information she sought.

"I'll leave you to rest," Lady Moreton said. But before she quit the room she added, "I shall look forward to your company at dinner."

Caroline's mouth dropped open as the door closed behind her ladyship. She span around trying to take in the sheer luxury of the room. She could hardly believe where she was, in the home of Lady Moreton, to whom she was a complete stranger, being pampered and cosseted, but why? Catching a glimpse of herself in the glass she sneaked a mischievous grin. "If I am exposed to anymore surprises today, I shall go completely distracted."

But she couldn't settle. Not only had several days in the carriage made her stiff, but also she was used to walking around the cove, taking the sea air and feeling the wind on her face.

A loud bump outside her room dispelled her thoughts of the sea. There followed a knock.

"Enter," she called.

A maidservant, several years older than the girl from the inn, entered the room followed by two menservants carrying the sea chest. They men deposited their burden and left.

"Shall I unpack Miss?" the maidservant asked.

"Where is the girl who accompanied me?" Caroline asked.

Momentarily the maid looked puzzled. "Oh, do you mean the girl with the odd accent wearing a brown cloak and bonnet?"

"Yes, have you seen her?"

"Mrs. Hobbs, the housekeeper took her into her room as soon as she appeared in the servants' hall. The next I heard she was she'd been taken in the dog cart to meet the Stafford mail coach. I can only guess she was anxious to get home, Miss."

Caroline thought for a few moments. The girl had been a willing worker. She had looked after her at every inn and remained cheerful without speaking out of turn. A sense of loss welled up inside her. During the five days they travelled together in the carriage, she had welcomed the girl's company. It saddened her that she had been given no opportunity to say thank you or goodbye to her but she hoped the girl had been rewarded for her work. She would have to ask the Colonel for further particulars if she had the opportunity to speak to him privately. "Yes, unpack please and help me into the blue gown."

"At once Miss."

Having changed her gown, Caroline put her bonnet and travelling cloak back on. "I'm going to walk in the grounds."

"Yes, Miss."

"Can you show me to a side entrance?"

The servant led her downstairs to a door which she pushed ajar.

"Thank you, that will be all." Leaving the girl Caroline slipped through the gap which led to an inner courtyard. Crossing the yellowed flagstones she passed under a turreted archway and gained access to the outer walls of the hall. To her left were the stables, best avoided, she decided as she walked over the cobbled yard towards a large wooden door. Pushing it open, she slipped through into a formal rose garden laid out in six large rectangular beds. But it was too early in the season for blooms, although the bushes were neatly trimmed and the beds well-tended.

The crunch of gravel beneath her feet reminded her of pebbled beaches near home. Home, she thought, she no longer had a home. The sound of a clock striking the hour broke her homesick melancholy. She left the formal garden and strolled towards a grey square tower which she assumed was the chapel. The path was pleasantly tree-lined and the leaves had just burst their buds, young, fresh and green. Halting she inhaled and filled her lungs with spring air. The large chapel door looked inviting, a welcome sanctuary? It was tempting to lift the iron latch and go inside, but today she craved open air and wide sky, so boldly she strode into the parkland.

"Are you sure she is Henry's daughter?" Lady Moreton asked.

"I had sight of the parish record and have a copy signed by the parish priest, Reverend Mr. Hawkins, likewise for Henry Moreton's death, or should I refer to him as Sir Henry, for had he but known of his brother's death he could have claimed both title and estate."

"There is no need to remind me. We knew nothing of him," his mother said. "I did not wilfully prevent him inheriting. It was *he* who turned his back on his kin."

"Why?" Richard asked anxious to know as much about the late captain as possible.

"I don't know exact details but it was something about his choice of wife, I believe." She turned away from him as she spoke, flicked open her fan and began wafting air towards her face. "During his final months Sir William spoke little and what he did say hardly made any sense. 'Henry will take command,' he said repeatedly but made no indication of where or how we could contact him. As you know William was a broken man after Waterloo and I don't know what I would have done if it hadn't been for your support." She gave him a sympathetic smile, then closed her eyes and shook her head.

Richard stiffened. He hated any reminder of the day his young half-brother was cut in two by cannon shot. He blamed himself. Charles had always wanted to be like him, although he had tried hard to convince the young man of the cruelty of the battlefield. But Charles only saw what he wanted it see. At nineteen, filled with the wonder and adventure of youth, he saw only the glory of war and probably believed himself invincible on the battlefield. "Why Charles wouldn't believe me when I told him about the hollowness of victory and the stench of death I do not know."

"My dear, if I have told you once I have told you a thousand times, you must not berate yourself over Charles' loss. I was his mother, as I am yours and I do not hold you responsible."

Richard felt his chest tighten, as it always did when his half-brother's name was mentioned. But no matter what absolution his mother gave, he still held himself culpable.

"How much does she know?" Lady Moreton asked but received no reply. "Richard, I asked how much-"

"Forgive me mother, I heard you the first time," he replied and turned towards her. "On first acquaintance Miss Moreton appeared meek and kept her own counsel. Either she is a good actress whose talents are wasted here, or totally ignorant of her station and inheritance."

"And she is not promised in marriage?"

"I understand the captain and his daughter were well-respected in the village but did not venture into the neighbourhood. I suspect Miss Moreton has experienced little of society. No doubt you will soon be changing that."

"And pray why should I expose an innocent flower to the ravages of society? We must stand together on this matter and protect her from fortune-hunters. Or have you forgotten our plan?"

"No mother your scheme has not slipped my memory. And Sydney, what do you propose for him?"

"The title is his so he'll have to be content with that."

"And when he discovers we have kidnapped his cousin?"

"We have done no such thing. Caroline came here of her own free will, she is my guest."

"And what happens when she discovers she is a guest in her own house?" Richard raised a cynical eyebrow, inside he was fuming, his mother's plotting sat ill with him. "How much do you intend to impart to the meek Miss Moreton?"

"I shall tell her who she is, but not that she is the Moreton heiress. As far as she is concerned I hold the estate in trust in my husband's name. That is all she needs to know."

"And what if Sydney turns up, like the bad penny we know him to be. He'll soon let the cat-out-of-the-bag if he thinks he can turn it to his advantage."

"Then you must not delay. Weston Grange will not keep you in the manner to which you have become accustomed. You know you cannot marry without some attention to money, despite your principles."

"And what might those be?"

"Oh, Richard, you are so like your father, do I have to spell your virtues out for you?"

"If you must," he whispered in a half-breath, knowing his mother would do so anyway.

"Honesty, integrity and fair-play," she counted on her fingers.

"And what you would have me do is neither honest nor fair."

"But it will solve all our problems," she pleaded. "Think of your own estate."

Richard didn't need his mother to remind him of the sorry state of his affairs. He had badly neglected his small estate whilst he fought for King and country.

"You're thirty in October," Lady Moreton persisted. "You should have a family of your own and indulge your dear mother with grandchildren. Besides with the two estates united we can all live comfortably."

"But not in the same household."

"Of course not all being well."

It was her last words which bothered Richard. He didn't like his mother's plan. The girl was innocent and what better way to protect her than to marry her. Could he convince himself he was acting in her best interests or was his motive a purely selfish one. Her image flashed before him and her green eyes stayed with him for several minutes.

The hour for dinner arrived too swiftly for Caroline. As she rested in her room after walking in the grounds, there was a tap on the door and the maidservant who had attended her earlier entered.

"What's your name?"

"Brown, Miss."

"No, your Christian name."

"Jane, Miss."

"Will you be attending me during my stay, Jane?"

"Yes, Miss, but please call me Brown. Then all the other servants will have to call me Miss Brown, now that I'm a personal maid. Miss Wilson says so."

"And who is Miss Wilson?"

"She is her ladyship's personal maid and she is training me."

Caroline thought for a few moments, having never had a personal maid in Devonshire, it felt quite strange to have another person taking care of her personal belongings. But she didn't want to send Brown away if it would cause the girl embarrassment below stairs.

"Very well, I've already laid out the white muslin. Can you help me dress?" With Brown's help, it didn't take long to change gowns.

"Would you like me to dress your hair, Miss?"

Brown asked.

Quite capable of arranging her own hairstyles Caroline was unsure what to say, but decided to let the maid do her best with her long blonde tresses. Living a parochial life she hadn't adopted the current fashion of short hair. Her father had likened the style to that of a cabin boy when she had shown him a sketch taken from a London fashion plate she had borrowed from the vicar's wife.

Brown began by brushing each long handful of hair. Then she produced a length of narrow blue ribbon. "Miss Wilson gave me this, she said the colour might suit you."

Caroline smiled at her reflection in the glass and was delighted with the maid's skill in coiling ribbon around pinned curls. The final result made her look very ladylike, she decided as she admired her reflection.

"Thank you, Brown," Caroline smiled. "You have done a grand job."

The maid grinned. "Perhaps Colonel Weston will notice you Miss? Downstairs the maids think he's ever so handsome."

"Does he live here?"

"Oh, no Miss, he's got his own estate close by but visits often to discuss matters with Mr. Oakley, the steward."

Their conversation was cut short by a tap on the door. Brown answered and returned to say Lady Moreton requested her attendance downstairs and the footman was at the door ready to escort her.

The double doors of the library were opened

for Caroline to enter. It was a large long room, lined with books with a huge stone carved fireplace.

Lady Moreton sat in a large winged chair near to the fire."Do sit down, my dear," she pointed to one of the nearby settees.

Caroline sat down on the edge of the seat, keeping her back rod straight. She felt she had entered an inquisition, where Lady Moreton, however polite and well-mannered she might appear, was determined to examine her closely. Despite the warmth from the blazing fire, she pulled her shawl around her shoulders.

"I hope you are not feeling the cold, my dear, but I can see you are very wise to bring your shawl. One can never be too careful at this time of year, warm one minute and cold the next. Now it appears you know little about us. What can we have been thinking of? Please forgive my son's churlishness, for I gave him strict instruction when I sent him to escort you. Of course, I would have come myself. But I am a poor traveller and Devonshire is so far away."

On hearing the colonel was her son, Caroline breathed a sigh of relief but hoped Lady Moreton didn't notice. If she did she didn't remark upon it.

"Richard," Lady Moreton called to the far end of the room. "Stop skulking in the shadows and find Miss Moreton some refreshment."

Before Caroline could decline the offer, he was standing before her with a glass of wine in his hand. He looked very distinguished in close fitting white breeches and a burgundy velvet coat. As she took hold of the drink, their fingers touched briefly.

A ripple of excitement ran up her arm. Her cheeks grew warm and she feared he would notice. The only way she could recover some degree of composure was to look away.

"Lady Moreton," she began unsteadily, "thank you for inviting me to your home."

"You are most welcome and I would have invited you sooner had I but known of your existence. My family is small and to discover such a delightful addition to our circle as you makes me feel the obliged."

Caroline felt her brow crease slightly, she didn't understand especially as nothing was turning out as expected today. But her curiosity had been aroused and like hunger was inwardly demanding satisfaction. "Please do not tarry with me, your cordial hospitality has been all generosity and if you would but explain our connection, then I would be the obliged."

"But my dear, surely your father offered you some explanation regarding his kin?"

"Lady Moreton please forgive my directness but I must speak plainly, I would not wish you to think I am here as your guest under false pretences. On his death bed my father begged me to send a letter to Moreton Arnscote. The letter was sealed, I did not open it. Two weeks later I received your invitation, if we are related then please explain our connection."

Lady Moreton straighten her back and raised her chin as if she was about to make a grand announcement. "Your father, Captain Henry Moreton was a younger brother of my late husband Sir William Moreton. I am your aunt, my dear, by marriage."

"But Papa never spoke of his family, I always assumed he had none."

"Miss Moreton," Richard drawled, "your father probably had his own reasons for silence. Most likely we shall never know, however, I hope you will make your own judgement with regard to your relations."

Caroline turned to face him squarely as he sat opposite her. "Colonel Weston can I assume we are cousins?"

"Richard is my eldest son from my first marriage, my dear," Lady Moreton said. "Although I suppose he neglected to tell you the connection." She eyed her son suspiciously, "You are the very devil, sometimes." Returning her attention to Caroline she explained her subsequent marriage. "Unfortunately, Sir William and I lost our only son at Waterloo."

Caroline sensed a deep loss in her aunt's words." My sincere condolences, your ladyship. England lost many of her fine sons in that great battle. I remember my father reading the reports to me. But from this day, if you will permit, allow me to share your loss. Although I have not had the pleasure of acquaintance with a blood relation before, other than my father, it is surely my loss too. I am sure he fought bravely."

"He did," Richard said, "and fell at my side. But you have another living cousin."

"Do I?" Caroline remarked, family revelations beginning to overawe her somewhat.

"Yes, Sydney Moreton is very much alive. I saw him in London recently. He is the son of James

Moreton, your father's youngest brother, alas also deceased. Sydney is your blood relative," he added, "whereas I am not, I assure you."

She felt his steel grey eyes boring into hers as he spoke. The feeling was keen, as if he was looking through a portal into her soul.

.

CHAPTER THREE

Throughout dinner Caroline received no respite from Richard's penetrating scrutiny as he sat directly opposite her. She ate slowly, savouring each mouthful of the delicious food. Besides, it would be most ill-mannered to attempt to speak with a full mouth. Perhaps that is one lesson she would have to teach her charges when she secured a governess position. She had not spoken to Lady Moreton about her plans for employment. It was too early in their acquaintance. Doubtless there would be ample time to explain her position when she had a clearer notion of exactly what Lady Moreton had in mind for her.

Observing her aunt's demeanour Caroline became increasingly convinced that behind the elegance lay a character not only used to getting her own way, but also prepared to go to any length to achieve it. Although she had only known the lady for a few hours she had decided Lady Moreton would be a formidable enemy.

As for the son she could not make out his character although she had given the matter much thought. He had remained aloof during their journey north to Staffordshire. There had been only one occasion when he had given her the opportunity to enquire about the Moretons and she had expressed no interest. He had not repeated the offer. Was this indicative of a flaw in his character, insensitivity to the feelings of others, or did it merely suit his purpose whilst travelling? He kept his distance once he had hired the maidservant and rode on horseback throughout the remainder of their journey. When they stopped overnight at inns, he ordered her meals to be served in her room. She hadn't questioned his actions as she had no right to do so. Hence, he remained a curious enigma. However, she wished he wouldn't watch her so closely.

When Lady Moreton suggested they retire to the drawing room, Caroline followed and expected Colonel Weston to remain for a glass of port and a cigar, as her father had often done in the small room they had used for dining in the cottage, whilst she sat alone in the sitting room. However, as she glanced quickly over her shoulder she found the colonel had not resumed his seat but was following them.

When they reached the drawing room Caroline sat down in the chair her aunt indicated, Colonel Weston took a seat at a small table and began reading from a volume that had been lying there. That he was at a distance from them pleased her but she could still feel his enquiring eyes boring into her.

She looked around at the room, which new to her. It was spacious. The furniture was opulent, gold trimmed and in the Italian style. On the walls hung large paintings depicting scenes from the Continent, possibly a collection acquired from a Grand Tour during the last century. The room impressed her greatly having only seen its like on a brief visit to Bath when her father had sought medical advice after falling ill.

"My dear, I must tell you something of the colourful history of Moreton Arnscote.," Lady Moreton said. "The original house was fired by Cromwell's troopers during the Civil War, but we were most fortunate that the family were able to build the present hall. How it must have risen phoenix-like from the ashes during the Restoration."

She spoke quietly and with great feeling, which left Caroline in no doubt as to the enormous affection Lady Moreton had for the family seat.

"This is indeed a remarkable house," she said. "I would welcome a tour when it is convenient."

"Yes, of course, my dear, I am sure Richard will be only too pleased to show you all the nooks and crannies, won't you?" She called over her shoulder to her son, who raised his head briefly from his book and acknowledged his mother's request.

Caroline didn't look in his direction, she feared her cheeks might pink, or worse, they would turn flame red. Inwardly she was annoyed with herself for allowing her emotions to rule her head. But why did the man have to be so attractive?

"Moreton Arnscote had always been a very romantic house," Lady Moreton said. "It has such a happy ambience. Why when the boys were young..." Her voice drifted away.

Richard rose, strode towards his mother and placed his hand on the shoulder. "Do you play and sing, Miss Moreton?" he asked.

"A little," Caroline replied and dared to glance up at him. "However, I would not press my talent upon others. My father preferred a game of chess and with no male company in our household, I was press-ganged into chess service."

An amused smile danced across his lips and softened his face. "Bravo, Miss Moreton," he said, "I do believe we shall make a wit out of you yet." He crossed the room and returned with a box under his arm. "Would you like a game?" His engaging smile revealed a perfect set of white teeth.

Perplexed, Caroline didn't know what to say, she hadn't expected to exhibit her playing skills so early into her visit and least of all on the chessboard. She had played against her father for as long as she could remember, but bar a few games with the Rev. Mr. Hawkins and the local squire, who both called upon her father regularly, she had never challenged anyone else.

"Please play Caroline," Lady Moreton said, "for I swear Richard gets quite bored here with my company, although he won't admit it. I have never been able to master the game of strategy despite Richard's best efforts to instruct me."

Left hardly any choice, Caroline kept to a defensive game plan until she could judge the colonel's measure. He too, played a tight game, she noted, until perhaps flattering her ego, he left a knight unguarded. She concluded he had intentionally made a bad move. Why? To test her? Patronise her? Did he want her to win? If so why? The irrational move cut across his measured run of play. She took the advantage to turn the game in her favour and mated the colonel's king in four moves.

"My goodness, Richard, have you lost? Why I cannot remember the last time. Charles could never-" she broke off, emotion choking her words once more. "If you'll...excuse me," she muttered and stood up. "I...must retire."

Colonel Weston quit the games table, rushed to his mother's side and placed his hand at her elbow. He said a few words to her, but Caroline couldn't hear what passed between them. She busied herself collecting up the chessmen and put them back into their box.

Meanwhile the colonel escorted his mother into the hall. Caroline heard voices but again was too far away to hear what was being said. She had half-crossed the room about to leave, when the colonel stepped through the doors and closed them behind him, leaving the footman outside.

Caroline glanced around uncomfortably, they were alone.

"You're not retiring yet, are you?" he asked.

"I believe I must. It has been a long day." She sighed in an attempt to fake tiredness, although aware her senses, sharpened by the challenge of the game, were too acute for slumber.

"You must grant me the satisfaction of a rematch," he said standing between her and the door.

"Perhaps tomorrow?" She stepped to the side but he mirrored her movement.

"No that will not do," he said firmly. "You're not tired, are you?"

Caroline noted how his voice had softened to a

gentle cajoling tone.

"It's an excuse, isn't it?"

She made no answer alarmed how easily he read her inner thoughts. His steel grey eyes searched hers as he spoke.

"What are you afraid of?" A rakish smile creased the left side of his face. "Me? Or the revenge I might extort from you on the chessboard?"

The challenge made, Caroline rose to it. The cowering little mouse charade she had been hiding behind was played out. She prepared to flex her lioness' claws. She looked him straight in the eye. "One game Colonel Weston and play to win."

A muscle twitched nervously along his lower jaw but he made no reply.

It was a long game, vying one way then the other. Outwardly Caroline remained calm, or hoped she did, inwardly she was using several days of pent up frustration being cooped up in the carriage. Her mind thrived on the intense concentration the game provided. He was a worthy opponent, she decided, equal to her father but eventually she had him cornered.

"You have left me no escape route," he said, "what a general you would have made on the battlefield."

"If that is a compliment, then I thank you. My father taught me to play. He was the master, I merely the student. It is your move."

He reached for his king and brought him down. "I resign for I have no desire to hear your declaration of Check Mate twice in one evening. Well done, Miss Moreton, your skill is admirable, do you play cards as well?"

She realised he was teasing her and didn't wish to engage in verbal banter. "The hour is late. I must retire." She rose and made for the door.

He came after her and blocked her exit with his arm against the panel. Before she could object his hands were around her upper arms pulling her towards him. "I want you, Caroline, I wanted you the first day I set eyes on you when you opened your cottage door to me."

She gasped, felt her cheeks flame and feared he was in earnest. "I don't understand," she said.

"Don't you?" He pulled her closer.

Now he was so close she felt his hot breath on her cheek. She wanted to cry out but his lips descended onto hers and silenced her. Overwhelmed by his kiss, she felt powerless. Her senses aroused, strange sensations vibrated through her body. For the first time in her life she felt the pressure of a broad male frame against her body. His strong limbs seemed to burn through the delicate muslin of her gown. It felt as if the cold mask she had hidden behind all evening was melted by the warmth of this previously unknown physical contact.

Had she wanted him to take her in his arms? Had her actions asked for his touch? Had she secretly been craving the comfort of a man's embrace? But all she was aware of was his closeness. She could feel him, smell him and taste him.

She had no notion of when or how her arms moved to cling to his broad shoulders. His fingers gently stroked the back of her neck and loosened the blue ribbon which held her locks. Blonde curls tumbled about her shoulders and her pulse raced as he caressed and kissed her throat.

"You mustn't..." she stammered and pushed him away, confused by her reaction to him and her wantonness.

"Mustn't what?"

"Kiss me," she panted and stepped back. Guilt swept over her, painful guilt at the stark realisation of what had occurred between them. Ashamed of her inability to resist him, what had come over her? She had never kissed a man before and been kissed...it was too much.

Free of his embrace, the urge to flee was all powerful. Desperately she wrenched open the door and raced towards the stairs anxious to reach the sanctuary of her room. Not once did she look back. When she reached safety she slammed her door behind her and remained panting behind it for several minutes until she was certain she would be left alone. Only when all fear had drained from her did tears of shame spill down her cheeks.

Richard stared through the open door, what had he done? Slowly he retreated inside the library, picked up a decanter of malt whisky and poured himself a generous measure. He hadn't meant to test her and treat her nothing better than a doxy he might have met at Vauxhall Gardens. He felt ashamed at having taken advantage of her.

The first glass he drank had no effect. Why had he felt the need to try her and gauge her reaction to a male advance? For a few brief moments he thought he had succeeded in shattering the mask she hid behind. Then he realised, she was an innocent and what he had done in those few moments would be sufficient for any father or brother to demand that he act honourably, or face the barrel of a pistol on the duelling field.

Would he tell his mother? He shook his head. With her emotional character, the servants, the neighbourhood and half of the county would know of his despicable behaviour towards the innocent Miss Moreton and he would be left with no alternative but to marry her.

But wasn't that exactly what his mother wanted? To his shame the answer to that question was yes.

He decided not to tell her what had happened between him and Caroline. His stubborn nature would not let him play into his mother's hands so easily. However, as the second glass of scotch burnt its way into his stomach, he knew his goal had to be marriage to Caroline. Otherwise Arnscote would fall into other hands and his mother into his. He couldn't explain why living with his mother was intolerable to him, perhaps guilt over Charles' death? If only the boy had lived to become Sir Charles Moreton, then their mother's attention would be firmly fixed on the younger son and the enigma of Miss Moreton wouldn't have crossed their threshold.

Although he couldn't bring Charles back, he could save the Moreton estate by marrying Caroline. Her face flashed before him. Those engaging green eyes looked up at him and he remembered the softness of her skin. Perhaps marriage to her wouldn't be such an encumbrance.

However, his third glass of whisky cast doubts on his plan. Had he frightened her away by his action? Somehow he had to curb his lust and behave in a more gentlemanlike manner. Miss Caroline Moreton had to be wooed.

Caroline awoke early the next morning determined not to be drawn into a compromising situation with Richard again. Initially she had blamed herself for what had occurred between them, but on further reflection she decided he must shoulder the major portion of the culpability. His behaviour had not been gentlemanly.

Undoubtedly he was a rake and probably had a philanderer's reputation to match, but why, in the name of Heaven, had God made him so handsome?

The sun streamed into her room. She went to the casement window and opened one of the panes. The morning air smelt fresh and inviting, perfect for a walk. She dressed quickly in a plain grey gown and slipped on her thick leather boots to keep out the dew. Finally she draped her travelling cloak around her shoulders and tied the ribbons on her matching brown bonnet. She would exit the house through the side door the maidservant had shown her yesterday.

As she descended the stairs she passed a couple of footmen and a maid about their morning tasks. Doubtless she had been the talk of the servant's hall on her arrival, but today? From the meagre state of her wardrobe she would already have been dubbed a poor relation and, therefore, of little consequence. Whatever was said of her below stairs didn't matter, her problems were more significant than servants' gossip.

In view of what had happened last night, she anticipated her stay at Moreton Arnscote would become increasingly more awkward. Besides, she could not afford to ignore her distressed situation, perhaps Lady Moreton, whom she had considerable difficulty thinking of as her aunt, could assist her to secure a post as governess? She resolved to speak to her on the matter at her earliest convenience.

Descending the terrace steps she took the bridle path towards the chapel. Her pace quickened. If felt good to be outside and be at one with nature. The park appeared to stretch for miles and was attractively landscaped with a number of trees she had never seen before, especially the large evergreens bowing their branches to the soft green lawns. She was surrounded by acres of green, so very different from the wind-blown coastline where she had grown up. Between the proud pines, tall deciduous trees spread their branches, their leaves on the point of bursting to full summer glory.

Under the bright morning light a track through a shaded area of pine woodland looked particularly inviting, so she took it. Some distance along the track she thought she heard the thud of hooves. She turned to glance over her shoulder and spied a single rider some distance away. Quickening her pace she sheltered behind the wide girth of an oak tree.

The steed snorted as the rider reined in and

dismounted with a thud.

Not wanting to be seen, she shrank behind the oak tree and pulled her cloak around her skirts.

Footsteps approached. Her heart pounded. Afraid to look for fear of being discovered, she held her breath. Silence...painful moments followed as she craned to hear every movement, but her pursuer was playing the waiting game too.

A large damp hand grabbed her wrist and swung her around.

"Colonel Weston, you scared me half to death!"

"Don't walk alone," he snapped. "Take a groom or maidservant with you, even in the grounds."

"Whatever for?" she asked. "I used to walk for miles at home along the beach and through the countryside."

"You are a stranger in these parts, you do not know what danger might be lurking," he said his voice softening to a coaxing drawl. "If you had waited but half hour we could have ridden together and enjoyed each other's company all the more."

"I cannot ride and please let go of my wrist."

"Why? So you can run away from me again. We had important matters to discuss last night."

"Discuss," she cried. "Perhaps sir, I did not like your method of communication."

"Your aversion is noted, madam, but do not feel it implicit upon yourself to apologise to me. I am a man of the world, I fully comprehend."

"Apologise, I am the one who should be receiving the apology after...after your brutal assault on me!"

"Assault?" he laughed but still held on to her wrist. "I think you understand our communication well enough my dear Caroline." And with a lustful glint in his grey eyes, he lifted her constrained hand to his lips and kissed it.

Annoyed she brought her free hand up to strike him, but he blocked the blow before she could make contact with her target.

Holding her rigid before him he said, "How I like a woman with spirit."

His warm breath was on her cheek like the previous evening and she tried to turn away but could not prevent him stealing a fleeting kiss. His arm encircled her waist, his other hand held her head firmly. She could not escape the demands of his warm lips. Softly she stopped resisting and let the powerful sensations streaming through her body take full rein.

He let her go and stepped back, his eyes glistening above a broad smile.

"You, sir, are not a gentleman." She picked up her skirts and ran along the path towards the hall.

CHAPTER FOUR

Later in her room, having regained her composure Caroline wrote her journal. She wanted to know why, as a lost relative, her presence had been so earnestly sought. What can Lady Moreton want with me? She scribbled and tried to outline her feelings about the colonel, but the words wouldn't come. She sat at the writing slope her pen poised but her emotions were too raw, she could not commit her inner most secrets to paper.

She had changed into her blue wool gown, the skirts of the grey one she had worn for walking in the morning were muddied and she had laid it over the back of a chair in an attempt to dry the hem. The blue gown fitted her well enough and she added a white lace collar which had belonged to her mother.

There was a knock on her door and Brown entered carrying a breakfast tray. "The footman gave me this note for you, Miss, with instruction to be read immediately."

"Thank you," Caroline said as the maid set the tray down before her. "Can you manage to dry the hem of my gown?" She pointed to the grey dress draped on the back of a chair.

Brown looked at the gown. "Yes Miss, I'll take it downstairs and dry is over the ovens in the kitchen."

When the maid had left, Caroline broke the seal on the note. It was unsigned and requested her company in the study at ten-thirty to make plans for the day. She didn't recognise the hand. Her stomach clenched – could it be from the colonel?

He disturbed her because she couldn't explain her reaction to him. He had been the perfect gentleman when he escorted her from Devonshire, yet now, his behaviour had undergone such a material change she could hardly believe he was the same person. Which was his true character - the military gentleman or the rake who had kissed her? She blushed at the memory of their physical encounters, yet found the experience exhilarating. The realisation made her feel ashamed. Her reaction to him had been most inappropriate. She must not allow him to kiss her again but how was she to stop him? Once again she vowed she would not allow herself to be alone with him – but what if the note was from him? They would be together again and alone.

At the appointed time she waited outside the study. The footman opened the door and announced her. She still wasn't used to the household formality. What was the purpose of constantly being announced? However, perhaps it was a courtesy paid to guests and who was she to express her opinion? There were other more important matters to deal with. She screwed her fingers into tight balls as she entered the room convinced he would be present and possibly alone.

Her apprehension was confirmed. The colonel rose from his chair behind a large mahogany desk.

She looked away, preferring to look anywhere except at him. The study was new to her, although as her eyes scanned the dark oak panelled walls several portraits glared down at her. Her eyes rested on one picture which reminded her of her father.

"Your grandfather, Sir Henry Moreton," Richard said.

"Where is Lady Moreton?" she asked quickly not wishing to be alone with him.

"Mother may join up presently, but please be seated." He indicated a seat on the other side of the desk.

Reluctantly she took it, her fingers grasping the chair's arms so tightly her knuckles whitened. Perched on the edge of the seat, she was ready to spring up and make a hasty exit if he came any closer.

He resumed his seat and elbows on the desk he leaned forwards until his chin rested on his hands. "My observations of you since our first meeting tell me you are no fool, do you know why you were invited here?"

"Flatter me all you will Colonel Weston, however, I have no notion why Lady Moreton requested my company. The only circumstance which brought about our acquaintance was the death of my beloved father. And for my part I am beginning to regret sending his letter. I can only assume he requested Lady Moreton's help in some way as I have not yet reached my majority. But why he kept silent about his family all my life, I do not know."

He took a deep breath. "Your father and his

elder brother quarrelled. Alas, my mother and I do not know why. Apparently it occurred when your parents married, which was around the time my own father died. My widowed mother married Sir William. They had a son, Charles, who was born on the first day of the new century. Whatever breach occurred in the family, I assure you, my mother remained ignorant of it."

"And Charles fell at Waterloo?" She noticed how a muscle in the colonel's clean shaved jaw twitched at the mention of the battle. She expected him to reply but when he said nothing she added: "Sir William must have been a brave father to allow his fifteen-year-old heir to go to war. I thought soldiering was reserved for younger sons."

"Or older stepsons." He covered his face with his hands as if there was something he did not wish her to see.

Caroline thought for a few moments, she did not want to cause pain yet remembered her aunt's reaction the previous evening. "Last night Lady Moreton was upset when she absent-mindedly mentioned her son's name, I assume she still mourns him keenly."

He lifted his head and stiffened his neck. "Yes, it is close on three years but do mothers ever cease to grieve?"

"Probably not," she replied and thought of her father.

"Forgive me," he said the tone of his voice softer, "you are in mourning too, perhaps we best return to more pressing matters. Now we are acquainted with your circumstances, my mother wishes to give you the protection of her home and grant you the station in life a niece of hers could expect."

The offer of a secure home surprised her, but what would be expected of her in return? "That is very kind but I did not come here seeking charity. Lady Moreton's benevolence and generosity is beyond reproach, but she owes me nought. However, perhaps she could assist me in securing a post as a governess in a respectable establishment, as I wish to make my own way in the world."

"Miss Moreton...Caroline." He dragged his fingers through his long fair hair. "You are a gentleman's daughter, no you are more, don't you understand?" He did not wait for her reply. "For the past two years of his life your father was Sir Henry Moreton, the eleventh member of your family to hold the title, had he but chosen to do so. Thus, I fail to see how your interests or those of the Moreton family could be best served by you taking a teaching post!"

Annoyed by his rebuke, she glared at him. "Then pray sir, what am I to do?"

"Remain here, mother would dearly enjoy your company and may even be persuaded to give you a London Season."

"Season? I know nothing of London Society."

But there was no time to argue further, the door flew open and Lady Moreton rushed in. "He has come," she cried, "I am all of a flutter. Richard, you must stop him at all costs."

"Mother nothing is settled, nor will it be if that pompous ass is given free rein."

"But I thought-"

"Do not think, please mother. Go and attend to

your guest, doubtless he will need food and refreshment after his long journey."

"Why did he not inform us of his visit?" she wailed. "Instead he descends upon us to hang the sword of Damocles over our heads." She began to wring her hands. Richard moved from behind his desk, put his arm around her and escorted her to the door. He watched her cross the hall then closed the door. Turning back to Caroline he said, "Forgive the intrusion, my mother has a tendency to fluster, a touch of brain-addle, I fear, but she has a good heart."

His description of his mother's behaviour surprised her so much she began to wonder if the lady's mood swings were self-perpetuated or the consequence of life with her unpredictable son. Whatever the reason, she began to question what sort of establishment she had entered.

"I wanted to break this to you more gently," he said, "but it seems our visitor's arrival has upset my plan. Therefore I must speak plainly, your father died leaving considerable debt."

"Which I have discharged," Caroline returned quickly.

"Indeed and highly commendable, but your efforts were insufficient to clear his gambling debts."

"What?" she sprang to her feet. "What you are saying is intolerable. There must be some mistake. My father was no gamester."

He rose but paused for a few moments before speaking as if to choose his words carefully. "I'm afraid he was, but it is not my intention to cause you distress, or speak ill of the dead." He edged his way towards her. "Rest easy, my dear Caroline, all of his debts have now been discharged."

She began pacing as he spoke, then turning to him asked, "By whom?"

"I shouldered the responsibility," he replied staring at her intently. "I trust I was not too presumptuous. I acted in your interests and those of the family."

Annoyance, even anger started to well up inside her. How could she have remained ignorant of the circumstances until now? "When did this come about?"

"Shortly before I came to collect you from Lee Cove. I had been in the neighbourhood for a few days meeting creditors and arranging payment. The cottage could not be saved. The date for repayment of the loan raised against it had long passed. You were fortunate not to have been evicted several months ago."

"And how much did you have to lay down on my father's behalf?" Heat flared inside her as her heart pounded.

"Around two thousand pounds."

Her mouth dropped open and her hand flew to cover it. Tears well up inside her as reality struck her. It would take her a lifetime to settle such an amount, if ever. She turned towards him, blinking slowly to hold back the tears she was determined not to shed. She loved her father, to learn such intelligence of his character was bitter news. She lifted her head and clasped her hands together as if in prayer. "But...how am I? How is such a sum to be repaid? What is to be done?" she walked towards the window where she gazed across the neatly trimmed rose beds. "You must know there is no way I replay you."

"There is one way," he replied in a soft voice, "and it is why you are here."

Was his taunt a deliberate one? She wondered if it was another part of the cat-and-mouse chase he had been leading her through. Was it part of his plan to drown her in indebtedness then throw her a lifeline?

He approached, stood alongside her and said, "I have reached a time of life when I must think to marry. My own estate adjoins this one, but it is small in comparison and fell into sad neglect whilst I was away at the wars. I have been able to execute some restoration work but much labour lies ahead. To build an estate and a home a man requires companionship, a family and an heir."

Struck silent, Caroline's ears burnt. Was this a proposal? Whilst unprepared to hear his words they might explain his previous behaviour towards her. He had been testing her with his kisses. But they knew little of each other. Could one marry on so short an acquaintance? Her mind shifted over all their recent encounters, hopped from one meeting to the next until...she became confused. She shook her head as if to clear her brain.

"In short, Miss Moreton, will you do me the honour of becoming my wife?"

Caroline kept her gaze firmly fixed on the rose garden. "No, Colonel Weston, I will not."

"Why not?" he demanded. "I am not engaged to another and we are not blood relations." He stepped closer to her. "For Heaven's sake Caroline have the courage to turn around and face me!"

Determined to keep calm throughout her explanation she took a deep breath and turned towards him. The face she met was dark and foreboding, obviously her unexpected refusal had infuriated him. His mouth was set in annoyance and he glared at her, frowning. "I am in mourning," she said, "but if I were to consider your proposal, I would need to believe some affection existed between us."

"And my observations of the holy state of matrimony show the most successful marriages are between two people who are not hampered by passion of the heart."

"Indeed." The cynicism of his remark grated upon her. However, she noted how his colour had heightened. She turned away from him and started for the door, but he barred her exit.

"Think again Caroline before you walk away from me again. Why are you refusing me? You do not find my embrace repulsive, that we already know and I find you very attractive. Perhaps if I had declared my passion for you and proposed like a simpering youth in the first flush of love, you might have agreed. But you are no fool, think again. I am convinced we can deal well together." He drew in breath. "I am making you a good offer and this-"

She felt his muscular arms surround her as the weight of his body pressed against. His punishing kiss grazed the inside of her lip, a kiss she was powerless to stop. Her diminutive strength was useless against his tall, athletic form. How could she oppose him? Even the thought of doing so became increasingly futile. Her body came alive at his touch. Her skin tingled with sensations unknown to her before she had encountered him. As he kissed her, her mind fought for him to stop but her body yearned for his caress.

"You know you want me," he whispered, released his hold on her and cupped her face in his hands. "I want you too, as I told you last night, from the moment I laid eyes on you. I can't keep my hands off you."

"Why me?"

He brought his hands down onto her shoulders. "You are young and full of life. Dressed in fine clothes Society will adore you in London. I don't want to lose you to some worthless fop and stand by and watch him fawn over you. Please reconsider my offer."

She shook her head and made for the door, but he followed her. All she wanted to do was make her escape. As she placed her hand on the door handle, he covered it with his hand. The heat from his palm seemed to pass along the length of her arm. He was close to her again, so close she could feel his breath on the nape of her neck. If he embraced her again, she knew she could not resist him. Why did he make her feel this way?

"Please think carefully about my proposal, I am convinced we could deal very happily together once we were accustomed to each other's ways."

"Give me some time to think on the matter," she said weakly, blinked with bafflement - it was all too much to take in at once. She needed time alone, time to think and time to sort out her emotions.

"As you heard, Mother has a visitor, an

unexpected caller whom she does not welcome, but we must grant him hospitality. I hope he will not impose himself upon us for too long. It would be better if you stayed out of his way as he comes to discuss business affairs. Will you keep to your room until dinner? I'll have the kitchen send you some luncheon as Mother and I will be engaged with our caller. The man is bombastic, rude and crass, so do not be alarmed if you hear raised voices."

"Of course," she replied grateful to the unknown caller for unwittingly providing her with some breathing space. She didn't know the visitor's name but something cautioned her not to ask.

Richard watched her back as she ascended the stairs and disappeared from view along the gallery landing. Then he turned to Harris, the butler, ordered a footman to be stationed outside Miss Moreton's room and luncheon to be sent up. "Under no circumstances is Miss Moreton to leave the house. Do you understand?"

"Yes, sir," Harris replied.

Richard strode across the hall, signalled the footman to open the library door and went inside. Lady Moreton sat near to the fireplace and her nephew, Sydney Moreton stood over a large volume open on one of the library tables. He looked up as Richard entered.

"I've been trying to make myself at home," Sydney drawled with distinct mockery, "but seems my aunt has forgotten who owns this estate."

"I have done nothing of the sort," Lady

Moreton said. "You sir, arrive unannounced and have been received in a most cordial manner. That we have little conversation of consequence is because of your outrageous attitude and false claim upon this property. Thank goodness you have joined us Richard and can sort this matter out."

"Sort the matter out, madam, the matter requires no sorting. I have proof that Captain Sir Henry Moreton died a full month past. As the next surviving male Moreton, the title is mine. So, I'd be obliged if you, madam, and your son addressed me in the correct manner."

Richard looked at Sydney's portly figure, although his coat was well-tailored, his collar points were somewhat excessive as his double-chin was squashed between them. He had light brown curly hair and piggy eyes. Richard assumed he must have taken after his mother, for he could detect nothing of the strong Moreton countenance, high forehead or generous mouth in Sydney's face. "Sir Sidney," he began in a cynical drawl, "I trust you had a pleasant journey from London."

"Pleasant journey! Poppycock sir, no gentleman has a pleasant journey travelling north along rutted roads and staying in flea-ridden inns. And I did not travel all this way to engage in polite chit-chat with you. Sir Henry is dead and I gather from my man of affairs, my uncle foolishly laid no claim to his title or the estate. So, here I am, to stake my claim and take what is rightfully mine."

"But what about Caroline?" Lady Moreton asked.

"Caroline?" Sydney glared at her. "Pray madam, of whom do you speak?"

Unwilling to stand by and see his mother bullied, Richard advanced a few paces towards their visitor. "Sir Sydney," he began in a calm voice of authority, "we had heard of Sir Henry's death and mourn his passing, however, Moreton Arnscote is not entailed to the male heir. Sir Henry has a daughter and it was his dying wish that she should be placed under Lady Moreton's guardianship until she reaches her majority."

Sydney stood silenced for a few moments. A muscle clenched along his jaw, his eyes grew narrower and he shook his head. "I don't believe you," he cried, "where is your evidence? Where is this girl?"

Richard met Sydney's accusing eyes without flinching and rose to the challenge. "Lady Moreton has a letter from Sir Henry requesting her assistance in this matter. Miss Moreton is a legitimate daughter and the rightful heir to all her father's property and chattels."

Richard watched Sydney's face change. The man nearly turned puce as he clenched his fists. "And where is the young lady?" His lips twisted in a curved, stiff smile."I would very much like to be introduced to my cousin."

"I regret that won't be possible, Miss Moreton is not out yet, although I know my mother will be making arrangements for her niece's introduction into Society." He glanced at his mother as he spoke, hoping she would follow his lead.

"Caroline is young," Lady Moreton gave her nephew a thin, calculating smile. "However, when she does make her debut, I am sure she will be very popular, why we might even hope for an earl or dare I hint perhaps a duke?" She paused and gave her nephew a small, self-satisfied smile.

As Richard watched his mother carefully, he hoped she would not over-react to the situation. He had chosen his words, so at a later date he could not be accused of wilfully misleading Sir Sydney. However, he knew whatever he said, the news of an heir, and a female one, standing in the way of a large inheritance would not find favour in Sydney's quarter. The man had debts because he gambled too frequently and borrowed funds against the prospect of his imminent inheritance.

Sydney touched his lips with his forefinger, as if to silence the real words he wanted to impart. He stepped towards Lady Moreton's chair and bowed slightly before her. "But surely as her nearest male relation I should have been called upon to share in the girl's guardianship, if only to protect the family from fraudsters." He edged closer to Lady Moreton as he spoke, bending his back slightly in a simpering pose.

Immediately Richard noted the manipulative ploy and hoped his mother would see through her nephew as easily as he could. So he glared at her hoping she would not respond to Sydney's blatant offer of so-called assistance.

He breathed a sigh of relief when she said, "Before you proceed on your journey, Sir Sydney, won't you take luncheon with us?"

"But madam, I have arrived at my destination and have no mind to set off for London to-night. Four days on the road, madam, I am exhausted and so are my valet and two grooms. I had a mind to stay a few days."

She flipped open her fan and began wafting cool air over her face before replying, "I do wish you had written of your intention to visit, we are most inconvenienced."

Although silently praising his mother's handling of the delicate situation Richard knew it was time to intervene before she let slip that Caroline was under their roof. "Sir Sydney, I think my mother did not intend to sound unwelcoming, however, we have engagements in the neighbourhood."

"Then pay no heed to me, I shall be no trouble, however, I assure you madam, I did write two weeks ago outlining my intention to visit, I cannot think what happened to my communication." He reached for a handkerchief from his cuff and began dabbing his nose followed by his sleeves as if to remove the dust from the road.

What is to be done? Lady Moreton eyes pleaded to her son. Richard took command. "Mama, Harris can arrange for suitable rooms to be prepared in the west wing for Sir Sydney and his valet."

"Yes, the west wing," Lady Moreton echoed. "I'm sure you won't mind overlooking the stables as we are renovating the guest rooms in anticipation of receiving my niece."

"Of course," Sydney replied, "and when are you expecting the young lady to take up residence?"

Lady Moreton again glared at her son.

"In June," Richard replied quickly and signalled the footman to call the butler.

Caroline's luncheon arrived on a large tray carried by a footman with Brown leading the way. The maidservant instructed him to leave the tray on the side table and closed the door after him. "Will there be anything else Miss?"

"Could you attend to a couple of marks on the front of that gown?"Caroline pointed to the white muslin she had worn at dinner the night before. "And if you could stitch some pink or green ribbon around the sleeves I think it would improve the gown greatly."

"Oh, yes Miss, I can do that immediately." She placed the gown over her arm and left the room.

Caroline ate as much as she could, but left some bread and cold meat. She took the napkin, placed the food in the centre and tied the four corners together. She laid out her spare blue woollen gown, placed the food, a flannel petticoat, shift, flat pumps and a pair of pantaloons inside, and bundled the lot together. With a small amount of money in her reticule, the blue bundle was all she could hope to carry. She laced up her walking boots, threw her brown cloak around her shoulders and tied the ribbons of her bonnet securely under her chin. She let out a long sigh of relief. She was ready to leave Moreton Arnscote for good.

As the chapel clock struck two, she left her bed chamber. Fortunately, the footman posted outside her door was slumped on a chair taking a nap. She hoped he wouldn't get into trouble as it was obvious he had been placed there either on guard, or more likely to prevent her wandering at will. The idea that she might be kept in her room forcibly by Colonel Weston's command vexed her, however, it if was his doing it only made her more determined to leave.

She slipped unobtrusively through the kitchen and left the house via the servants' hall. No one stopped or questioned her. She made her way along the drive and kept close to the trees as she didn't want to be seen from the house.

With each step she felt guilty about running away. It seemed so cowardly, but wasn't it her only option? How long would it be before he compromised her? Marriage, yes he had promised her that, but how many times had she heard of girls being duped by men of consequence promising them marriage? Why should he marry her? He wanted her, but would that want last as far as the altar? She doubted it.

And what of her feelings for him? Strange and mercurial - one moment she disliked him, then closed her eyes and pictured his handsome smiling face. And when she thought she never wanted to see him again, her treacherous body recalled the warm, strong embrace of his arms.

Escape provided her only logical alternative. At a distance from the residents of Moreton Arnscote, she would be free to make her own decisions.

Within half an hour she reached a small hamlet and assumed she had left the estate. A farm hand came towards her and doffed his cap.

"Where is the nearest inn and the high road?" she asked him.

"That be the Bull's Head, Miss, on the Stafford Road." He pointed in the direction she was already going. She thanked him and continued along the road.

She walked for most of the afternoon until the temperature started to drop. The countryside appeared deserted and with so little money, she began to question the wisdom of her venture. However, she pulled her bundle closer to her body and marched on.

About an hour later, she heard a rider approaching at full gallop. Anxious not to be seen, she stepped back off the road but missed her footing and toppled into a ditch. Her feet squelched in the cold muddy water as she struggled to climb out without letting go of her belongings.

The rider had reined in and dismounted for she heard the thud of his booted feet approaching. The sound grew louder until he was almost on top of her. Her eyes flashed up at him as he plunged into the ditch beside her.

The cold muddy water splattered up over her skirts and cloak. She ignored it and clung to her blue bundle. However, when his strong hand grabbed her wrist she tried to resist but her effort was useless.

The colonel pulled her towards him. "Come here," he ordered and dragged her out of the ditch, but failed to release her when they were back on the road.

"Unhand me, sir!" she cried as his steely grip tightened.

But he ignored her and marched her towards his waiting horse. Only when he turned to face her did he relinquished his grip on her wrist and slid his hands to her upper arms where he held her firmly. "You silly fool!".

She struggled in his grip. "Remove your hands from my person," she demanded and shot him a determined look.

He released her, turned away and untied his horse's reins. He patted the animal and spoke words of comfort to him in a low voice.

She glared at the back of his head, annoyed that he spoke to his horse more gently than he addressed her. "By what right do you pursue me?" She demanded and clung to her bundle as if her life depended upon it.

He turned to face her and shook his head. "Have you run mad? Alone, out here, I had no other course but to follow you. You are in my mother's care."

As he stood before her, tall and angry, the force of his reply took her off-guard. "How did you find me?" she demanded as her heart lurched madly.

His expression bordered on mockery. "John Turney, he's a good man, thought it odd to see Lady Moreton's house guest out alone."

"But...how does he know me? I only passed a few words with him and I certainly didn't tell him where I had come from," she said defensively.

His mouth twisted into a sardonic smile. "You will have to learn that not much passes unnoticed on the Moreton estate. Actually, you are trespassing on my land and judging by the condition of your clothes, it is fortunate we are near to Weston Grange."

A warning voice whispered in her head and unfamiliar tension started to grip her chest. His house was the very last place she should go. "I have…no wish to go there," she stammered her misgivings increasing by the second.

He looked at her as if he was dressing down one of his staff. "The choice is no longer open to you. You cannot return to Moreton Arnscote in your current dishevelled state. It is but half a mile to the house from here. I will help you to mount."

"The horse! I cannot ride."

His eyebrows arched. "Then allow me to escort you, Miss Moreton." He held out his hand but she refused to take it, instead she clung to her bundle. "Miss Moreton please do not behave Missish and pretend to be offended. It would be unseemly for us to arrive back at Moreton Arnscote together and the only way we could do that is to both ride my horse, and don't say that no one would see us. Come to my home where you can rest and make good your apparel. Then you can return by carriage with a servant."

She thought for a few moments, her madcap scheme to escape her aunt's grasp had failed. She shivered as the muddy ditch water squelched in her boots. She stole a glance at him and became keenly aware of his close scrutiny of her. "Very well."

No words passed between them until they reached a gate alongside the road. "We can cross the high meadow," he said. "It will shorten our walk by half." He unlatched the gate and opened it sufficiently to allow her and the horse to pass through.

She didn't speak but acknowledged his action with a demure smile. Within a short while a large timber-framed house of the Tudor period came into view. Weston Grange – his home. The sandy mellow hue of the plaster and timber framing was bathed in the early evening sunlight which glistened on the leaded window panes. The house looked welcoming despite several visible signs of neglect.

"This way," he strode ahead leading the horse into the stable yard where he called for assistance. Two grooms rushed out of the stable offices and one led the horse away.

"We did not expect you, sir," the older groom said.

"And I did not anticipate returning today." He turned to Caroline, "Come my dear, this way to the house. You have had a long walk and must be in need of refreshment."

She felt his hand at her elbow as he guided her across the yard. He sounded very sure of himself and she began to wonder if she would be returning to Moreton Arnscote tonight. The thought worried her as she began to feel like a bird with its wings clipped, unable to fly free.

"When will I be returning to Moreton Arnscote?" she asked as they passed under the archway and turned towards what once must have been a formal garden but now overgrown.

He removed his guiding hand and stepped in front of her. "I hoped we might have this conversation inside the house in private, but as you insist upon it. You can return when I have your word that you will not attempt such a foolish venture again. My mother offered you hospitality, a roof over your head and how do you repay her, by running away." His vexation was evident from his tone.

"I wasn't running away from her," she said emphatically. "I wanted to put distance between us and now...now I am here."

"Oh, am I so much of an ogre to cause you to embark upon a somewhat desperate venture?" he asked smoothly in a mocking tone, his expression taut and derisive.

"I am not going to marry you," she said but found she could hardly lift her voice above a whisper. Since he had pulled her out of the ditch, she had gone over and over in her mind what she would say to him when he asked the real reason for her flight. There was no other way, she had decided, to meet his massive and self-confident presence other than to face him directly with the truth.

But was it the truth? Her head resented the way he had treated her when they were alone, the stolen kisses, the touch of his skin on hers, but her heart? The feelings he had aroused in her were like nothing she had experienced before and would...could marriage add to her physical pleasure? Perhaps, if his promise of marriage came to fruition, but how could she trust him? He had settled her father's debts, or so he claimed, and in return wanted a closer link to the Moreton family to link the two estates when his mother passed on, for surely she would will the land to her sole surviving son. Did he feel guilty about potentially being the heir? And offering her marriage placated his feelings. His feelings? Did he have any emotional connection to her other than family guilt? She wanted to ask him but her lips were pressed shut.

"Very well," he shrugged with a heavy dose of sarcasm in his voice. "I assume you do not want to return to Arnscote tonight or any other night for that matter. Also you wish to be gone from here with utmost expediency, but as you appear to be in need of money I'll hire your services for the next few hours. For it would be most inconsiderate of me to let you leave the neighbourhood at this hour and without funds."

"What do you mean?" she asked half in anticipation, half in dread. The confidence she had had upon leaving her aunt's house had already waned. What were his intentions?

"Come with me," he ordered. He gave her no time to reply, grabbed her arm and escorted her through a rear entrance into the house. Via the servants' stairs they emerged in the middle of a long wooden panelled gallery. He marched her half way along and into a large room on the corner of the house with windows facing south and west. The last of the evening sun was sinking behind the trees.

She looked around her, inwardly cursing her naivety. "This is your room, isn't it?"

A broad mischievous smile crossed his face. "Where else can we have the privacy decorum dictates we need? What pet name did your father call you?" He shrugged off his top coat and threw it across a chair.

"You are impertinent sir." She cried and stepped back a couple of paces.

He raised his eyebrows. "I think not. Caroline is too long so I shall call you Caro. It suits your sharp wit and romantic nature."

She felt her colour deepened. As he had so easily struck upon her father's favourite name for her, what else did he know about her?

"How old are you Caro?" he teased, advanced towards her and pulled one of the silk ribbons on her bonnet. The bow untied but she didn't answer. "Of course, it is so improper of me to ask a lady's age, but I'd say eighteen." He brushed his jaw thoughtfully. "Let me see, you and Charles were born in the first year of the new century. I'll pay you eighteen guineas." He untied his cravat. "A handsome price but money well spent, it'll give us both a chance to discover what might have been."

Her heart had started pounding the moment he had dragged her out of the ditch, but now it was thumping so hard she felt it would burst out of her rib cage. "If you violate me in any manner, I shall have you charged by the magistrate. You have already committed a crime by bringing me here against my will."

He chuckled and tilted his head on one side."Caro, I really like the way you amuse me. Squire Talbot is an old family friend. He'll be told the truth that I found you in a ditch and rescued you, so don't start making up wild stories about me. You came here of your own free will."

"But I had no choice, you said that yourself. And won't Lady Moreton be worried when I do not return tonight?"

"She already knows that I would bring you here, once we had your direction."

Caroline looked up at him, realising she had played directly into his hands when she foolishly left Moreton Arnscote after luncheon. "Is your mother involved in this too? Am I supposed to feel so grateful that I fall helplessly into your arms?"

"I did offer you marriage. Many young ladies would have leapt at the offer." He pulled off his cravat, discarded it and began unbuttoning his shirt.

"But I'm-"

"My dear Caro, I've explained my reasoning," he insisted and took a step closer to her. "And mother has given her consent for you to marry."

Caroline frowned. "By what right does she have authority over me?"

"She is your legal guardian and can make you a ward of court until you reach your majority if you decided to run away again."

The thought that Lady Moreton, however kindly she might appear, had legal control over her left a bitter taste in her mouth. How had this come about without her knowledge? But would the position of a married woman be preferable? Then he, her husband would have authority over her person, goods and chattels – she would have nothing of her own. She stared blankly at him, words refusing to form on her lips.

"As for marriage, I regret to inform you that once you have spent a night beneath my roof, what is left of your reputation will hardly prove a fertile ground for suitors. In short, madam, your running away this afternoon has sealed your fate. You are already ruined."

His words stabbed her heart as surely as if he had plunged a dagger into her chest. She blinked several times to hold back the tears as she realised what he had said was true. Her eyes glazed and she fumbled for her handkerchief to prevent tears spilling over her cheeks. "Are you still offering me marriage?" she asked.

"You agree?"

All she could manage was a low affirmative response but it was a sufficient signal for him to take her into his arms. She did not resist, there was a strange relief in his strong embrace, comfort in the warmth of his muscular body next to hers. After a few moments she said, "I will marry you Colonel Weston, but I will be a virgin when I stand up in church to make my vows." She spoke with conviction, although she felt none of the joy she had expected to feel on accepting her first marriage proposal.

"My dearest Caro, you have my oath on it," he said followed by an irresistibly devastating grin. "A servant will be sent with the news to Arnscote immediately."

"And when can I return there?" she asked.

"On the morrow for you need only stay beneath my roof for one night." He gave her a conspiratorial wink.

"Stay the night!"

"Oh, do not fear, my dearest Caro, you can trust me not to lay a single finger upon your delightful person. I have given you my oath and whatever else you might think of me I am a man of my word. Tomorrow we will journey to Arnscote together in my carriage, announce the news of our engagement and I will leave you in the care of my my mother, whilst I call upon the bishop in Lichfield."

CHAPTER FIVE

Caroline gazed disbelievingly at her reflection. The bride before her looked radiant, her gown presented to her by Lady Moreton claiming it had been hers when she married Richard's father. The gown was indeed a work of art, but very dated evidenced by its richly embroidered velvet and brocade fabric, wide skirt and accentuated narrow waistline. The striking colours would contrast with her light blonde hair, but ruby red and gold were hardly the hues she would have chosen herself. White muslin and Empire style with a dark blue or green spencer and matching bonnet would have served admirably in her humble opinion. But Lady Moreton would have none of it and insisted that the ruby and gold gown would pay an excellent compliment to Richard. Caroline had doubted that because since he had returned her to his mother's care, he had hardly spoken to her. So why would he pay her the slightest attention even when their wedding day arrived?

That day had come and she stood before her glass with a hint of sadness in her green eyes. Today she missed her father. If only he were here, she wouldn't be marrying Colonel Weston or playing a leading role in the Moreton charade.

Several times over the past few days she had resolved not the go through with the ceremony. She would escape. Thoughts of freedom had never been far from her mind since she had given him her consent. But her plans had always ended in despair. It wasn't possible. He would surely find her and bring her back again.

Perhaps some of her anxiety might be eased if he showed a hint of affection for her? But he hadn't touched her since he had brought her back to Arnscote. To him she was a convenient arrangement although he hadn't said so. She assumed his mother's conscience had been placated as she had done her duty as an aunt and found her charge a suitable husband. As for the colonel, he must have secured a sizable dowry from the Moreton estate, for she could think of no other mechanism that had tempted him to marry her. "How can a wedding be arranged so hastily?" she had asked him a few days ago when he explained his plans for the ceremony.

"The legal aspects have been settled." He grinned like a Cheshire cat and added, "I've obtained a special licence from the bishop in Lichfield. We will deal well together."

The hour of the wedding approached. When she looked into her glass she didn't recognise the young woman dressed in a vibrant gown of the last century. Her fingers tingled as she clenched them tightly until her nails dug into her palms. She took a deep breath and forced herself to relax. Another wave of uncertainty swept through her and gnawed away at the last shred of confidence she had left. How could she marry a man she barely knew?

But she had to, she had given her word and he had given his. Gingerly she put one foot in front of the other and picking up the skirts of the heavy gown she stepped out of her room.

From the top of the stairs she looked down at the small party waiting below. Her heart beat quickened, her temperature soared and she felt as if a hand was closing around her throat. She focused on the top of Richard's fair hair tied back with a gold bow and her stomach knotted with nervous anticipation. He looked up at her and she felt impaled by his purposeful, confident gaze.

He moved to the foot of the stairs and held out a welcoming hand. She descended slowly, unaccustomed to the weight of the heavy gown. In contrast he appeared every inch the military officer, resplendent in his regimentals and devilishly handsome. Under his arm he had a dark leather box.

"I have something that mother wishes you to wear today." He opened the box revealing its contents. A necklace of brilliant blue sapphires surrounded by diamonds sparkled on the black velvet upon which they lay. "The Moreton sapphires."

Caroline swallowed deeply, she had never seen more brilliant gems and although she had no way of telling whether they were genuine or fake, it hardly seemed to matter. He lifted the necklace from its case and held them out to her.

"Please allow me to fasten them for you," he said.

She managed a brief nod as he placed the jewels around her neck and closed the clasp.

They felt heavy and cold against her skin, what a decorated doxy she must have looked, she thought, who wore red, gold and bright blue sapphires to her wedding?

"There, you make a wonderful bride. I shall be the envy of every man present," he said in a self-satisfied voice.

She wanted to reply but a suffocating sensation tightened her throat and prevented her from doing so. If only she shared his confidence as they began their journey into what would inevitably be a loveless marriage, or at least that is how she perceived their situation. However, she had been left in no doubt as to her role in the nuptial charade. Provide a legitimate heir and, in exchange, she would receive an establishment, a name and security. Was this all a gentlewoman could aspire to?

Her eyes filled with self-pity. He cared nothing for her, yet what did she feel about him? He disturbed her emotions, was that love? Strange tingling sensations ran along her arm when accidently his hand brushed hers. Was that love? Whenever he entered a room she felt the place was dominated by his presence and his presence alone. What that love? When he quit a room, she felt empty, yet she despised his conceit, his arrogance and his insensitivity. Could she mellow him? Perhaps, so was that love?

Time had run out. She took a few steps across

the hall in the heavy gown and felt drawn by his eyes to him. His smile for her looked like one of genuine admiration and for the first time that morning she felt a surge of joy in her heart. But were his actions merely part of the charade in which they had the leading roles?

When he offered her his arm, she took it. "I am much pleased you have decided to enter the chapel on my arm," he said and led her to the door. He inclined his head towards hers and whispered, "Together as we intend to go through life."

Drawing in breath, she felt anger flare inside her. Why did he have to be so cynical today? She held her breath and made no reply to him, preferring to suffer in silence. Thus they quit the house and walked the short distance to Moreton Chapel.

Dozens of faces turned towards her as she entered the chapel on Richard's arm. News of the nuptials had spread rapidly especially as all the labourers and tenants from both estates had been granted the day off to celebrate the union. Estate workers and their families had gathered along the driveway which swept up to the hall and cheered as the couple passed by.

Quickly they reached the altar steps and the vicar was addressing the congregation with the familiar phrase, "Dearly beloved..."

Caroline took little of it in. Her head filled with doubts, had she really considered what marriage to a man like Richard would entail. What would he demand of her? If his actions so far had been merely a taste of what was to come, she held her breath but it still wasn't too late, was it? Would she have the courage to decline? Would she be able to speak out with the chapel filled with neighbours and well-wishers? What would her father have said?

She closed her eyes. *Papa would never have allowed me to get this far to the altar if I had misgivings about the alliance.*

Her bridges were burnt as Richard's positive reply to the vicar's question about taking her as his lawful wedded wife echoed in her ears. The vicar spoke to her. She swallowed allowing herself a brief moment of hesitation and felt the words well up inside her. "I will."

It felt as if another Caroline had spoken as Richard slipped the ring on her finger. The blessing given, the licence and the parish register signed. It was done. They were married.

They emerged from the chapel into a bright April day. Richard dropped a brief, affectionate kiss on her lips and arm in arm they walked back to the hall. But not a word passed between them.

Nearly everyone knew Lady Moreton and her son but few knew the bride, hence being introduced to so many people Caroline found it impossible to remember who they all were. She felt isolated and her heart pounded an erratic rhythm. Although Richard kept close to her side and played the devoted and adoring bridegroom, few words passed between them. Throughout the ordeal she felt that if she stumbled on even one syllable of polite conversation, her husband and his entourage would descend upon her.

Eventually Richard whispered for her to withdraw, indicating it was time for her to change from her borrowed bridal gown into simpler travelling apparel for their journey the five miles distance to Weston Grange.

As the door in the bed chamber closed behind her, she breathed a huge sigh of relief. At last she had escaped from the pressure of constant scrutiny by people she didn't know. Liberated from every inquisitive eye and out of earshot for a few minutes, she gazed at her mirror. The girl in the red and gold gown with the brilliant sapphires around her neck didn't look so different from the one she had seen earlier. Her eyes remained tinged with the same sadness but now she was joined in holy wedlock to a man she hardly knew. Now she was Mrs. Weston. She closed her eyes and imagined him at her side, tall and strong with his powerful, muscular chest hot against her gown.

Brown entered and helped her remove the old-fashioned garment and heavy necklace. She changed into a much more comfortable gown of cream silk gown with a blue velvet spencer and matching bonnet. As she was putting on her gloves, there was a light tap on the door.

"See who that is," Caroline said half-guessing it was Richard.

As he entered the room, she caught his reflection in the glass. He had changed his clothes too, from bright red colonel's uniform into a more sober coat of dove grey. His attire, from his cravat to the high gloss of his riding boots, was a credit to his man. However, from the cut of his coat to the elegant finish of his pristine linen in Caroline's eyes he was the supreme example of predatory male – a rake. Was this the nature of the man she had married? The question stabbed her heart, did she care more than she had allowed herself to believe?

She saw him eye the necklace and almost as if he read her thoughts he said, "Regretably, the Moreton Sapphires must remain here, although I doubt if they have ever graced a more pretty neck."

"You flatter me sir," she replied.

"And cannot a bridegroom flatter his bride on their wedding day?"

"Of course," she conceded.

Torn by conflicting emotions she descended the stairs on the arm of her new husband and glided through the assembled crowd of smiling well-wishers.

He assisted her into the chaise and taking the reins urged the horse on. Finally she was alone with him, but her heart wasn't singing as she had expected it to be on her wedding day. There were too many questions left unanswered. From their first meeting on her doorstep in Lee Cove to standing up with him in church today, it had all happened too quickly.

It had not been without seeking explanation, but she had been fobbed off with excuses, largely given by her aunt who had taken up the greater part of her time arranging fittings for the new wardrobe. Such had been Lady Moreton's demands that a team of seamstresses had been brought to Moreton Arnscote to complete the work.

But now they were alone. Her ears burning and her nerves on edge, she could delay no longer. She turned to him. "Why have you married me?"

He didn't reply immediately, which annoyed her. He kept his eyes fixed on the road, but she noted the nervous flick of his jaw muscle. Eventually he said, "Do you really want to know?"

His question vexed her. "If I did not require a reply, Colonel Weston, then why would I waste breath asking?"

He gave her a brief side-glance, as if the tone of her question surprised him, but when his face creased into a self-satisfied smile, she realised sarcasm would probably be futile with him, besides cynicism was not part of her nature. It was also sufficient to convince her that whatever he said next would be in jest.

"Mrs. Weston," he drawled, "I want you."

It was not the answer she had expected, however, from the beginning of their short acquaintance she had found his behaviour difficult to predict. As for his mood, that was mercurial, a character trait she attributed to his mother. "For what purpose?"

"To bed," he exclaimed seeming to rather enjoy the joke.

Her body heat rocketed as she struggled to control the spasms of alarm erupting within her. How would her wedding night unfold? So engulfed with embarrassment she remained silent until they reached Weston Grange.

"Come along, my dear," he said matter-of-factly, "let me help you down."

She did not expect his hands to clasp her waist so tightly or his gaze to travel so intensely over her face and search her eyes. Her heart jolted and she tried to stop the sizzling current racing through her. When he put her to the ground, his hands lingered around her as if he was claiming his rightful possession. The flame she saw in this eyes startled her and she tried to back away. However, something intense had flared between them, but she didn't understand what it was.

"Do not be afraid, my dear Caro, I have no intention of pouncing on you the moment you cross our threshold. Please allow me a little more sensibility to your feelings than you appear to have accredited me."

With his hand on the small of her back he guided her towards the house and announced that she was to be shown to her room. His words surprised her, yet she didn't fail to catch the sarcasm in his voice and realised he was fencing with her.

"You will forgive me, my dear, but I must see my horses. One of my best mares was about to foal when I left this morning." Not waiting for her reply, he turned swiftly and left.

Caroline's mouth dropped open. The abruptness of his departure had surprised her, yet as she watched his broad shouldered back putting distance between them, she found the respite from his company brought her a measure of relief. She made her way to the upper floor where Brown was waiting for her. "I hardly expected to be abandoned on my wedding day," she said to the maid as she removed her bonnet and gloves.

"I understand the colonel is most attached to his horses, ma'am, and takes prodigious care of the breeding. It is said that his stable is one of the finest in the county."

"I wish I knew more of horseflesh, but alas my understanding is as meagre as that of the battlefield. However, if we were to speak upon ships and naval matters, I think I could claim some expertise for a lady due to my father's instruction. Alas, for all my knowledge and upbringing on sea-faring matters, it seems ironic that I have married an army officer."

Several hours later, Caroline took her seat at the dining table opposite her new husband. He had changed from his wedding clothes into a simple dark green coat, white cravat and buff pantaloons and black Hessians. His sudden appearance in the drawing room had surprised her, largely because she had no idea what to expect. She had sat there, alone gazing around the well-furnished, yet slightly forlorn room. The furnishing had been elegant, now they looked tired. Some of the blue silk damask covered chairs had worn seats and the walls were darkened by years of smoke from the large marble fireplace. But before she could think of what improvements she might suggest to Richard, the doors flew open and he entered.

Perhaps it was his dramatic entrance, or his pristine appearance that surprised her. She didn't know, except her heart slipped a beat.

Their conversation was muted, polite but meaningless comments. The only time he displayed any enthusiasm was when she asked about the mare. His face lit up when he proclaimed that he had great hopes that the new foal would be as handsome as his sire.

Caroline blushed, would any son she produced be as handsome as his father? But she didn't dare voice her silent question as a strange uneasiness began to engulf her. Nervous anticipation or fear of the unknown?

She picked at her food throughout the meal and moved vegetables and meat around her plate with little purpose. Her appetite proved non-existent.

In contrast Richard ate heartily. "Weddings make men eat," he said, "don't you agree?"

In no mood for conversation she replied, "I wouldn't know. I have only attended a few weddings in our parish. The bride and groom left for their new home direct from the church and the congregation retired to the Fisherman's Arms, the village inn. My father would not allow me to set foot in the place, so he took me home. However, he would often go there and return late at night three sheets in the wind."

Richard laughed. "I would have liked to have met your father, he seems to have been blessed with a better sense of humour than his elder brother, who could be somewhat crass at times. Of course, mother never saw that, indeed she would never have a rum word said about the man. But he did have rather fixed opinions. But why have you eaten so little? Is the meal not to your liking?"

"The food is fine. The fault is mine perhaps it is a bride's prerogative?"

"As a mere bridegroom I cannot answer for brides, but weddings do make a man hungry, especially when it's your own nuptials. Take my word for it." He reached for the platter and helped himself to another generous portion of roast duck.

In contrast, she abandoned her meal and sat

back in her chair. Hidden from his sight, she turned the gold wedding band around on her finger and became increasingly uneasy about what was to come. In silence she watched him eat heartily.

"Shall I retire to the drawing room and leave you to your port?" she asked when the last dishes were cleared.

"There is no need," he replied and turned to the butler. "Saxton, we'll take coffee in here."

"Yes, sir, at once."

Waiting for the butler to return, the regular tick of the mantel clock resounded in her ears but its fingers seemed to race around the face. The retiring hour would soon be upon them. Then what would she do?

When Saxton returned with the coffee she refused to have any. Instead she rose and said, "I shall retire now. Good-night Colonel Weston." She knew she sounded abrupt but her nervous state did not allow her to do anything except make a hasty retreat.

He stood up. "My dear Caro, surely it is time you called me Richard?"

She did not reply but hurried away to the safety of her bed chamber fixed by the thought that her sanctuary would probably be of short duration.

CHAPTER SIX

Richard sat down and Saxton poured him a small glass of port. The ruby red liquid tasted rich and he was glad they had saved a bottle of his father's best for this special occasion but disappointed Caroline had left so abruptly. It must have been a trying day for her, he thought, yet he could think of no other way to save both the estates. Perhaps he had been wrong not to inform her of her inheritance, but what would have been the outcome? His mother could have argued that she was her guardian, but if Sidney had insisted on his entire inheritance, could he have prevented Caroline from marrying? Or heaven forbid, married her himself. Sydney had doubtless borrowed against his future inheritance several times, so what would he do now the Moreton heiress was married?

The question left a bitter taste in his mouth. Yet when he thought of her a wonderful feeling of warmth spread through his body. Desire? Yearning? He recalled the brief kisses he had largely stolen, her bright eyes when she greeted him at that bare Devon cottage and her resolute defiance until she realised the father she had admired throughout her life had held secrets from her. He had never spoken about his family or his reasons for abandoning his birthplace.

The vicar, Rev Mr. Hawkins, whom he had spoken to before collecting Caroline, had portrayed a very different man from the father she held so dear. She appeared genuinely shocked by the revelation of her father's gambling debts, a matter the vicar had soon made him aware of as money was still owing to several men in the parish. How Captain Moreton had been able to conceal his gambling from his daughter remained a mystery. She did not seem a gullible person but love and family loyalty can blind the most intelligent of people. Perhaps Caroline believed what she wanted to believe.

And now he was holding vital information from her. The feeling did not run easy with him. He felt guilty and selfish. He had deceived her using monetary necessity as his excuse. If the Moreton inheritance was lost to them, his mother would take up residence at Weston Grange, he would have to sell his entire stable and survive on his army pension and the income from his small estate. Life would be possible but not comfortable.

So he had married her in the full knowledge that all she stood to inherit was from today his. It could all have been so different if Charles had lived.

He signalled for Saxton to pour another glass of port and drank it quickly. The red ruby liquid did not take away the guilt he shouldered. He signalled for another glass which he sipped. Charles was gone, nothing could bring him back, he owed it to his mother to help keep her in the manner his half-brother would have been able to provide had he lived. But at what cost?

Caroline was his and in truth he found her delightful, intriguing and yes, in his heart he had to admit, he felt deeply attracted to her. Had it been those green eyes which held his on the threshold of her cottage that first set him off? Or the soft touch of her lips? Perhaps the thought of holding her strong youthful body in his arms and making love to her? Icy fear twisted around his heart. How could he ever expect to win her love when she discovered his part in the Moreton inheritance deception? He had deceived her by concealing the truth from her and guilt was stabbing at his heart.

When Caroline entered the bed chamber, Brown was waiting for her. "You looked lovely today madam, everyone remarked what a handsome couple you made."

Caroline smiled at her reflection but did not reply as the maid helped her into the night attire Lady Moreton had insisted she wore. Seated at her dressing table, she reached for the hairbrush and handed it to the maid. Carefully, Brown stroked her mistress' golden tresses and tied them in a series of bunches with white ribbon.

"That will be all," Caroline said, holding her hands together to stop herself trembling. After Brown quit the room she had no idea of how long she sat in front of her glass. The nightgown covered in lace was too ornate for her taste, but it had been a gift so she thought she ought to wear it.

The day had been a whirlwind, from the

moment she began to dress for the wedding until she arrived at Weston Grange. Why had Richard abandoned her for his stables? Did he consider the birth of a new foal more important than the woman he had married?

Was he trying to give her time to adjust and to begin to feel at home in her new establishment? She glanced down at her wedding band, what would her life be like as Mrs. Weston?

Her thoughts drifted back to Lee Cove and her father. What would he have said about today? Would he have regarded the colonel as a suitable son-in-law? Regrettably, she would never know the answer, but perhaps he would have asked her about her feelings for the man.

My feelings?

The question sent a cold shiver through her yet it was tinged with mixed emotions. Part of her felt an awakening of excitement as she began a new journey on life's path, but inwardly she felt unsure. Her father had never mentioned or spoken to her about the day she might marry. He had never broached the subject with an affectionate, "When you are married and have your own children." Why had he never discussed her future, even when he was on this death bed? He had gripped her wrist tightly and made her swear to send his letter to Moreton Arnscote. Was his dying wish a desire to make good what he had done in his life? He must have known he was in debt, far greater debt than she had ever imagined, so was his dying wish his final desire to make amends to her and his family? The Moreton and Weston families have been joined before in matrimony and they are joined again. *But how do I feel about him?*

Silently she answered her own question. He excites me and makes my heart beat faster. Is that love? I blush sometimes in his presence and want him to look at me. Is that love? He is the most handsome man I have ever seen. Is that love? When he held me in his arms and kissed me the most wonderful sensation streamed through me and shortly we will be alone together. This time it will be different because we are man and wife. Will that be love?

He is conceited, arrogant and far too good looking. He is a soldier, a man of the world, why would he ever feel any affection for me when there must be so many other women he could have?

She didn't know how long she sat before her mirror. She didn't move until she heard the door handle turn. His footsteps approaching...she turned to look over her shoulder at him.

He wore a long robe over his white nightshirt and carried a bottle and two fluted glasses in his hands. Carefully he set the bottle and glasses down on her dressing table. "Wine, now or after?" he asked coyly.

Was it his cynical attitude, his deliberate taunting or just him? "No, nothing," she blurted scarcely aware of what she said.

"Tut, tut, afraid you might derive pleasure from our passionate union?" he chuckled.

"You'll expect me to enjoy it, I suppose," she replied.

"If your temper matches your passion, then I have no doubt of it," he said smoothly, "especially as I like a woman of spirit. There's something empowering about the fire in a female heart."

His flippant manner annoyed her. "You are full of conceit and egotistical."

He laughed and poured himself a glass of wine. "If that is your knowledge of my character upon our short acquaintance, I fear what you might think of me after tonight. Indeed madam, I warrant you'll call me worse afore the cock crows." He raised his glass to her in salute and downed the contents in one go.

She felt she had lost the first skirmish of the battle. Perhaps she should have traded on her innocence and thrown herself on his mercy? No, her spirit returned. She would not demean herself. True she had no real notion of the marriage act but she had no intention of confessing so to him. Her pride was all she had left. He should respect her purity and treat her accordingly.

But would he? Could she trust him? She feared his anger and the physical pain he might inflict upon her. She was aware from her home village of men who beat their wives, and knew wives had little redress. Was that to be her lot?

Behind her facade of pride there was a frightened girl, alone in the world, facing a husband she hardly knew, yet...she longed for the comfort of his embrace.

Almost as if he read her thoughts, he took her into his arms. Her first reaction was to wrench herself free, but his powerful hands were on her shoulders, holding her fast.

"Some men find reluctance intriguing," he said.

She nearly asked if he was one of them but

knew she didn't want to hear the answer if he said yes.

"Let us dispense with this," he said, released her and removed his heavy robe. Then he reached for her.

She moved out of his way, stood up and retreated across the room but backed into the bed. As the hard edge of the bed frame caught the back of her thighs something unleashed within her. Stiffening to the challenge, she sixed her eyes on her hunter.

In one swift movement he wrenched his nightshirt over his head and threw the unwanted garment across the room. All thoughts of running away left her head as he stood before her. His muscular body was beautiful, broad shoulders tapered to slim hips and...she blinked several times, her mouth dried at the magnificence of him. She had never seen a man in his prime completely naked. She forgot the edge of the bed, tried to take a step backwards and collapsed onto the bed.

Quickly he followed her, lifted her into the middle of the mattress and covered her with his strong frame. She closed her eyes as his plundering lips descended on hers claiming possession. With the weight of his naked body on hers, to continue to oppose him was madness, but to surrender would wound her pride. Slowly, she closed her eyes and allowed calm to flow through her body.

Breaking the kiss, he rolled to her side and began tracing the edge of her neckline with his finger. His single digit burnt a trail between her breasts as he eased the silk ribbons apart.

She opened her eyes. Aware of the maleness of

him, a combination of strong broad bone covered with smooth honed muscle, she marvelled at the mellow hue of his skin glistening in the candlelight.

His lips dropped butterfly-like kisses over her face and neck, as his hand began to caress her calf and thigh with feather-light tenderness beneath her night attire. Slowly he created a sensual path down between her breasts and exposed them. She flinched but he did not relent and lowered his mouth to tantalise the tip of one nipple until it responded to his physical embrace. Then he sort the next burgeoning peak.

Her nightgown was no longer between them and she gasped as his plundering lips moved lower down her body. The degree of intimacy he took racked her with disbelief. She tried to speak, but only a husky moan came out of her mouth.

A pistol shot cut the air. "God's teeth," he cried, "that came from below and I am unarmed."

Caroline gasped as the sound of several pairs of heavy footsteps bounding up the stairs approached. Another shot rang out, louder, closer and the door flew open.

"Pray God cousin, I am not too late!" a man bellowed from across the room as he advanced towards them brandishing a pistol. "You blackguard Weston," the man declared. "You'll not get away with this, I've brought the magistrate!"

When Caroline awoke the next morning her head throbbed. Who was she? Mrs. Richard Weston or Miss Caroline Moreton,?

Panic welled in her throat. How could her

father be Sir Henry Moreton? And how could she be heiress to the estate without knowing it?

In the confusion of the bed chamber she couldn't remember what had been settled. She remembered Richard had been frog-marched away. Where was he now? It all seemed like a bad dream but the intruder, his men and the local magistrate had been real enough.

"My dear, your cousin claims you have been tricked into marriage and duped out of your fortune by Lady Moreton and Colonel Weston," Squire Talbot, the magistrate had said

"Cousin..." she remembered asking, "what cousin?"

She shook her head, she didn't care about her so-called cousin who had had the audacity to burst into her bed chamber only about her marriage. Was Richard her legal husband? The thought froze in her brain. True they had spent time in their marriage bed together and there had been a degree of intimacy between them, could there be more?

She didn't know, for no one had explained to her the exact duties of a bride on her wedding night. The Squire had begun his questioning, whilst she sat wrapped in bed linen after an enraged Richard had been roughly man-handled and taken away. To where?

"Madam," Squire Talbot had coughed, his head likely worse for the drink he had consumed at Moreton Arnscote following the wedding. "Did Colonel Weston force you to marry him?"

She remembered glaring at her inquisitor with cold silence, terrified the armed men would do Richard grievous injury.

"Come, my dear, you seemed in fine fettle this morning when you stepped into the chapel and I didn't see Weston with a blunderbuss at your back." He paused to laugh at his own joke but no one shared it with him. "And if my eyes d'ain't deceive me, we're too late. The deed's been done, eh? The knot well and truly tied, I'd warrant."

When she didn't reply, another man stepped forward, the one who had been brandishing the pistol at them. "Cousin," he had called her, "I came here in your best interest, to rescue you from an imprudent marriage and to ensure the Moreton inheritance went to the rightful heir."

It had all been too much of a shock for her, one minute to be falling into a new magical world of sensuality, the next to have that world overturned by the intrusion of a man who claimed to be her cousin. Richard had insisted the intruder meet him on the duelling field and that justice would prevail. Would it? Or would she be a widow as quickly as she had become a wife?

Unable to cope with the shock of her situation, she had demanded their withdrawal.

That was last night, now she forced herself out of bed. Without the help of her maid, she dressed in a simple muslin gown and tied her hair with a white ribbon. As she was struggling with the last of the curls she had piled on top of her head, Brown entered.

"Finish this," she ordered.

"Yes ma'am, at once."

Whilst the girl was at her work, she asked her if she knew where the colonel was.

Brown smiled. "In his room ma'am, but there's

two men outside with pistols and nobody is allowed inside not even his valet. There's a right row going on in the kitchen. I couldn't make neither head nor tail of it."

Satisfied she looked presentable, Caroline went in search of the Squire and the gentleman who claimed to be her cousin, but as she left her bed chamber, she walked along the gallery to Richard's room at the corner of the house. Two burly men armed with pistols were standing outside Richard's door. She turned around without speaking to them and retraced her steps.

Descending the stairs, she heard voices from Richard's study and without knocking went inside.

"Ah, fair cousin," the younger man said, "please accept my most humble apologies for the intrusion last night, but under the circumstances I was left with no option. Had I but heard of the wedding sooner, I would have hastened my journey and informed you of the despicable situation you had fallen into. But alas, intelligence only reached me in London two days ago. I swear no one could have made a faster journey than my good self."

Caroline stared back at him. He was taller than her but not as high as Richard. She noted his small piggy eyes, made even smaller by excess fat around his face and especially his jaw. His appearance was made even stockier by the high corners of his collar that seemed to act as a funnel into which his large neck was poured. His portly figure, more common amongst older gentlemen sat uncomfortably around his middle region and gave the fellow a very bloated appearance, so different from

Richard's Adonis-like frame. "I do not believe we have been introduced," she reminded him, if only to bring an end to his monologue.

"Forgive me, cousin, forgive me." He pressed his digit finger to his lips as if to silence himself but then pointed at her. "Don't you recognise me?"

"Should I? " Caroline replied and thought his manners rather rude. "Apart from the invasion of my privacy last night I have never seen you before in my life."

"No, no cousin, I meant family resemblance. My father, Sydney Moreton, always remarked how well I favoured his father, Sir William Moreton, our mutual grandfather. And now I have inherited the title from your father, you see before you your cousin, Sir Sydney Moreton, your most obedient servant." He bowed with a flourish.

His bow was over-dramatic, and for a few seconds she thought him rather foolish, but fools could be dangerous, especially as she had yet to discover what had happened to Richard. She feared her bridegroom had been injured, so she decided to deal lightly with her new found cousin. "Sir Sydney, I came to speak to Squire Talbot, perhaps I might have a few words with the magistrate in private?" She took a few steps towards her cousin and patted his arm. "I am sure you will find breakfast is being served in the small dining room." And she led him gently to the door.

"Of course, indeed," he said and a footman opened the door for him.

Caroline dismissed the manservant and turned towards the magistrate. "Squire Talbot, please tell me how you came to be summoned here last night, for Sir Sydney must have levied heavy charges against the colonel to bring you out." She took a chair and invited him to sit opposite her.

He sat down. "Indeed madam, the matter is somewhat of a delicate nature." He coughed loudly. "Sir Sydney claimed you were being cheated out of your inheritance by Colonel Weston who had duped you into marrying him in order to gain access to the estate."

Caroline frowned. "But surely the colonel has had *access*, as you term it, through his mother since Sir William died."

"Yes, my dear, but there was always the question of your father. They searched high and low for him, take my word on it. But if ever there was a man determined not to be found, it was the elusive captain. I knew him when I was a boy, you know. Always said he'd go to sea, and when the time came he insisted upon it. Fourteen he was, but Sir William, your grandfather, wanted him for the church. Young Henry would have none of it and he ran away to sea. Of course, Sir William then had to use a few of his connections and get him aboard a vessel as a mid-shipman. But there was not much love lost between father and son. Henry did well in the navy, but you know that I'm sure. He was a man's man, aye I'll say that for him, which is more than I'd care to say about Sydney senior."

"Sir Sydney's father?"

"Aye the same. Soft gutted he was. No stomach for sport or a fight, a pious fellow more suited to the church where his father sent him, although I'm not sure his manipulative character made him the best channel for the Lord's work."

The facts about her father's youth fascinated her because he had never shared any of his childhood memories with her. However, the news about the inheritance sat ill with her, but she didn't want Squire Talbot to know that she knew nothing of it until she had spoken to Richard. The realisation that she was the central key to the Moreton estate wounded her deeply and perhaps explained why Richard married her. Inevitably his mother had also been a party to the deception. But was it truly a deception? In her father's letter, what had he asked the Moretons to do?

"My mother, do you remember her?"

Squire Talbot shook his round face. "I'm sorry I knew nought of her, apart from the rumour that they were married in the chapel by special licence. Of course, it was said it was a private wedding. Sir William was opposed to it on account of the bride being foreign. He had already arranged a marriage for his second son. He cut your father off after that and we heard no more of him in the neighbourhood. Apart from a few despatches in the newspapers, he fought with Lord Nelson, didn't he?"

"Yes, I have a good account of the ships he served on and later commanded but I knew little of his early life."

"When news of young Charles' death came through from Waterloo, his father Sir William took it badly and never really recovered. At his passing, naturally there was talk about your father again. But no one knew where he was or whether he still lived. Most unfortunate."

He shook his head.

"What happened and who inherited Moreton Arnscote?"

"There is nothing like a death in the family and a disputed legacy to break a family apart. Regrettably, Sir Sydney, as he is now, but was Mr. Sydney Moreton, sought redress. He went to law and that can take a long time and be costly. The estate wasn't entailed, but when Sir William's will was read, he left the estate to his surviving brother Henry. As your father is no more, legally the title goes to Sydney, unless you have a brother?"

"No, I am an only child," Caroline replied.

"Now, did your father leave a will and has it been proven?" Squire Talbot folded his arms across his portly stomach.

Caroline thought of the debts she had settled on her father's behalf and what Richard had told her about the additional two thousand pounds he had laid out. "My father left a collection of papers, mostly his naval memoirs and accounts of sea battles. I have not read through all the documents. There might be a will, but I have not seen it."

"Then you must search for it, my dear, for if such a document exists it may have considerable bearing upon the Moreton Estate. As for Sir Sydney, he is determined to make you a ward of court. As your nearest blood relative he could claim guardianship over you."

Caroline's hand flew to her mouth as she let out a gasp. How could this be? Was she not a married woman? "What am I to do? Where is the colonel?"

"Ah! Last night Sir Sydney insisted the colonel be kept under lock and key."

"Upon whose authority?"

He gave her a sheepish look. "I am afraid upon mine as the local magistrate."

"But Squire Talbot, how can you stand by and let this happen to a man whose character you have known for many years. And Sir Sydney? How long have you had his acquaintance?"

"I knew them both as young boys, obviously living in the neighbourhood I had a better knowledge of Colonel Weston than Sir Sydney, but in my position I cannot allow personal preferences to influence me in legal matters. You must understand, my dear."

She did not like his patronising manner, especially when he kept calling her 'my dear'. Could he not bring himself to address her as Mrs. Weston?

"I do not mean to pry but I must ask whether the colonel forced you to marry him? Although, there were plenty of witnesses at the ceremony and you did arrive at the chapel together, there might have been some coercion beforehand, was there?"

Her heart sank, she could not tell him everything that had happened between herself and the colonel, but if she told her story a certain way, then she could easily convince him she had been coerced into matrimony. And if she had wished she could have refused Richard, she didn't have to marry him. However, the cost would probably have been her ruin. "No," she answered in a half-whisper.

"Capital," the squire smiled, "always knew Weston was a man of good character, 'though a bit hot at the card table. I blamed all those years with

Wellesley's lot. Then there was that dreadful business with Charles at Waterloo. Sir William took it very badly, and who can blame him? Only son and heir gone. Sad business, the boy was only fifteen. However, I'm glad that Weston can now put his bad fortune behind him. It's good for the neighbourhood too, for the Grange to have a bright young filly to take up the reins." He grinned at her.

"Last night, Squire Talbot, what was resolved?"

He shook his head several times. "Oh, dear, dreadful mess. A man don't deserve to be disturbed on his nuptials, bad form...bad form."

She was about to insist her question was answered when they were disturbed by a manservant who informed them the Moreton carriage was approaching the house. She went to the window and saw Lady Moreton descending. "My aunt has come to call and I anticipate she will not be in good humour. Please excuse me sir, perhaps we can continue our conversation later?"

"Of course, my dear," he replied his hands clasped behind his back as he paced the room. "If I can be of service to Lady Moreton, please ask. In the meantime, I shall be with the colonel. I do hope he has had time to cool his heels since last night. He was all of a rage, but then who can blame him?"

Caroline did not offer her opinion instead she turned to the manservant. "Have Lady Moreton shown to the drawing room."

Lady Moreton marched into the drawing room where Caroline was waiting for her. "What an outrage!" she declared and dismissed the servant as if he was her own. She sat down before Caroline invited her to do so. "I always knew Sydney was a cad, but to force entry to a man's home and on his wedding night! What a meal the gossip-mongers will make of it. Think of the scandal. An outrage, it's the only way I can describe it."

"Lady Moreton," Caroline began aware her words might be hurtful, but her aunt cut in.

"I am unaccustomed to rising at such an early hour, but on receipt of Richard's note, I had to come, if only to reassure myself that all was well." She glanced around the room, "Where is he?"

"Squire Talbot has him under house-arrest-"

"Oh, my goodness, what has happened? Has he called Sydney out? Has anyone been injured?"

Caroline moved closer to her. "Aunt Margaret, no one has been hurt. I have not spoken to Richard this morning, Squire Talbot and his men will not allow it. However, I understand Sir Sydney is taking measures to make me a ward of court under his guardianship. Last night, he declared the wedding illegal and insisted that Richard and I be separated. But why? I do not have his acquaintance, although he claims we are related. What do you know about him?"

Lady Moreton pursed her lips before she spoke. "I thought you knew all about the family. Didn't Richard tell you our history when he brought you from Devon?"

Caroline shook her head, "No, but maybe it was because I didn't ask."

"Possibly but the fault lies with my son who can be somewhat contrary at times. But surely he explained the advantages of uniting the two estates?"

"He told me nothing of the estate," Caroline replied, her heart growing heavier every time she thought of him, which was often. "I desperately want to speak to him and hope his desire for communication matches mine, but the squire will not allow it."

"Squire Talbot is a bombastic old fool."

"That's as maybe, but it is Richard who is my concern. He said my father had debts which he had settled."

"And he spoke the truth. He did not lie to you. As his mother I assure you he is an honourable man."

"But he didn't tell me the whole truth, did he?"

Lady Moreton straightened her back. "I don't know what you mean."

"Then let me explain, when my father's letter arrived, you had confirmation of his existence and location. I do not know what he said, but you must have felt our family connection sufficient to invite me to stay. You sent Richard to collect me and to make enquiries in the neighbourhood. He discovered some of my father's debts had not been paid and settled them, for which I am grateful. But what he failed to do was tell me what is central to this whole marriage fiasco. My father inherited Moreton Arnscote from Sir William and I am my father's heir."

"But a young lady of eighteen years cannot inherit an estate. You have not yet reached your majority. Your father asked my husband and I to look after you, of course, he was unaware of his own inheritance and I suspect he knew nought of Charles' passing. I did not want to see you disinherited but the only way I knew how to protect you was for Richard to marry you."

"And by marriage, my inheritance passes into my husband's hands, does it not?"

"That is the way. It has always been so."

"Richard bought me for the two thousand pounds he used to settle my father's debts. It seems his investment will replay him many times over for Moreton Arnscote is worth well in excess of that sum."

"Caroline, a lady does not concern herself with monetary matters. We must leave those responsibilities to the gentleman. But how can you expect a gentleman of standing, talent and a hero of the battlefield to marry without some attention to fortune?"

"But you cannot deny you and he deceived me," Caroline blurted out.

"We did not," Lady Moreton insisted indignantly. "I had family and fortune to consider. I have made it possible for you to make a good marriage to a man who will respect you. So, Mrs. Weston, I suggest that you start respecting him as a good wife should."

"But Lady Moreton, what if I am not his wife?"

"Not his...what do you mean?"

"If I can prove he forced me to marry him, then I can have the ceremony annulled."

"Anulled," Lady Moreton gasped, "I swear I'm about to swoon."

CHAPTER SEVEN

Richard struggled to free his hands. The rope used to bind his wrists had cut red wheals into his flesh. His ankles too were similarly bound and he was dressed only in a loose shirt and three-quarter breeches. The only garments he had been allowed to cover himself with when he had been disturbed and ejected against his will from his wife's bedchamber. He had not slept. The rage fuming inside him had not been quelled even when dawn crept into the room where he was imprisoned.

Imprisoned! In his own house, he felt defiled. And where was Squire Talbot, his so-called friend and neighbour? He struggled again against his bonds to no avail. Seven years he had followed Sir Arthur Wellesley through the Iberian Peninsular and commanded a regiment at Waterloo and never had he been captured. Sir Sydney Moreton had a lot to answer for and he was determined to make him pay.

He heard voices outside the room and glared at the door. Whoever came through would know the degree of Weston fury and outrage before they opened their mouths.

"What is the meaning of this!" Richard shouted as Squire Talbot and Sydney entered.

"Now, now," the portly squire said, "couldn't do much else than tie you up. Sorry about it but there was no holding you last night. Why if Sir Sydney hadn't have brought his men with him, well there might have been murder done. And we can't have that can we, Weston?"

"Can't have? What are you spluttering about sir? This is my house you have invaded and I would like to know by what authority. As for you Moreton, you can sling your hook back over my threshold and do not set foot on my land again."

"Oh, dear cousin-"

"Do not claim any relation with me sir, we are connected only by marriage, an institution for which you have no respect. Be gone sir and leave me and my wife in peace."

Sydney's piggy eyes narrowed as a smile spread across his flabby face. "You know I can't do that Weston, the lady's reputation and fortune is at stake. Thus, as her nearest male relation, duty and honour bind me to act on her behalf, indeed sir, society would be a severe critic upon me if I did nothing for her." He took a few paces around the room.

"Stop parading in my house like some upstart French cockerel!" Richard said and turned to Squire Talbot. "I appeal to you as a friend, untie these bonds and hear my side of this bizarre situation."

The squire nodded. "But only if I can have your word as an officer and a gentleman that you will behave in a manner fitting your station. The circumstances we find ourselves in this morning are indeed unusual, to say the least, but you must appreciate as the local magistrate, I must act when informed of an infringement of the law in my neighbourhood."

"I respect your station," Richard replied, "and you have my word but I shall not take responsibility for my actions if Moreton remains on my land any longer than is absolutely necessary to resolve this misunderstanding."

"Very well." The squire instructed two of the men who had accompanied Sydney the previous night to free the colonel.

Richard leaned forward rubbing his wrists and stretching out his long legs. "Send for my valet. I need boots, coat and a cravat."

"Ugh! What a dreadful smell! Take it away, before I succumb permanently." Lady Moreton waved her hands in the air.

Caroline removed the bottle of smelling salts she had been holding under her aunt's nose and asked, "Are you feeling better?"

"Better...better? How can I feel better? Yesterday I witnessed my son marry and today his bride says she plans to have the whole ceremony annulled. I hear a very garbled account of what transpired last night that my nephew invaded your bedchamber and my son has been arrested. How do you expect me to feel? I want to know the truth, then perhaps I might *feel* better!"

Seeing her aunt had recovered her spirits, Caroline retreated from her position next to her to an adjacent chair. "I spoke to Squire Talbot and Sir

Sydney this morning but to little avail, they did not let me see Richard and I am worried about him. He was very angry last night when the squire arrived. It took several men to restrain him."

"Are you surprised?" Lady Moreton raised her eyebrows. "What an insult and the scandal? He will be the laughing stock of London society. Have you considered that? And what is this nonsense about an annulment?"

Caroline was about to answer when the door opened and Richard entered followed by Squire Talbot, Sir Sydney and his henchmen. Her stomach tied itself into a tight knot and she felt her cheeks pink but she couldn't take her eyes off Richard. His hair was tousled, his cravat hastily tied and his breeches creased, in sharp contrast to his highly polished boots and immaculate coat. By the look of his darkened jaw, he had not shaved.

His eyes sought hers and she felt her lower lip quiver. Was he remembering the touch of her skin last night with the same depth of feeling as she now experienced?

Along with the gentlemen Squire Talbot remained standing. "It falls to me to clarify some of last night's misunderstanding, although I find this a very peculiar affair." He turned to Sir Sydney, "Please state your case."

Sydney stepped forward. "Most certainly, Squire Talbot, as I related to your good self late last night upon arrival from London. Miss Moreton has not yet reached her majority and as her nearest male relative and head of the Moreton family, I am her guardian. But I find that she has been drawn into a marriage without my permission and considering that rightful ownership of the Moreton estate will soon be a matter of law, I had to act and act swiftly to save her from a most unsuitable alliance."

Caroline could hardly believe what she was hearing. The cousin, whom she had not met before last night was her guardian. And what was this about the ownership of the Moreton estate? She kept her eyes fixed on Richard, why would marriage to him be so unsuitable?

Squire Talbot coughed. "Sir Sydney, your cousin has married of her own free will, I was at the ceremony and I asked her that very question this morning. Now whether you consider her choice of a husband as unsuitable or not, it looks as though the deed has been done."

Sydney's colour rose above his high-pointed collar, his flabby cheeks swelling as his fury mounted. "No sir, I will not accept this situation until...until I have had the girl examined by a surgeon."

"How dare you Moreton!" Richard took two strides across the room to confront the man. "You're only interest in this matter is the Moreton estate, it has been your only interest since Sir William died and left the inheritance in question. You are driven by monetary gain. Firstly, I challenge your claim to guardianship over my wife, secondly, Moreton Arnscote is not entailed, Sir William was at liberty to leave the estate to whomsoever he chose and thirdly, you are trespassing on my property. Take yourself, sir, and your henchmen and leave."

A deep sense of pride welled up inside

Caroline as Richard spoke. A medical examination to ascertain her marital status filled her with fear. What would that entail?

Sir Sydney huffed. "No less than I expected of you Weston. Why your own estate has long been a parasite on Arnscote's back. What charms and allurements did you use to get the girl to the altar? Well, cousin Caroline? What did he promise you?"

"Sir Sydney, please refrain." The squire turned to Caroline, "Please, my dear, there is no need for you to answer any of his questions. Your evidence, anyway, cannot be taken into account, for it is known in English law that a wife cannot give evidence against her own husband."

Caroline breathed a sigh of relief, but her growing resentment of Sydney's presence and his accusations were beginning to cloud her judgement. What had Richard promised her anyway? His name, his estate...but could she trust him? She could not bring herself to answer her cousin's question and was relieved the squire had absolved her from doing so. But unanswered questions rested uncomfortably in her thoughts.

"Squire, may I speak?" The three gentlemen turned to Lady Moreton, who had kept a respectful silence since they had entered the room.

"Most certainly, your ladyship for I am sure you can bring some understanding to this apparent chaos."

"Sir Sydney, I know you have continued to insist upon your right to succeed to my late husband's title and I stood opposed to your claim. As it happens my judgement has been proven sound. Alas, we are now in mourning for my brother-in-law the late Sir Henry and I no longer stand against your claim to the title, indeed sir, I have just acknowledged you." She tilted her head in his direction and he responded with a slight bow. "However, as to the matter of my niece being made a ward of court, over that I have lawful objection. Sir Henry wrote from his death bed and begged me to take charge of the girl, *help to find her a suitable husband* were his exact words. So, as to Caroline's guardian, then gentlemen, I am her rightful guardian and in accordance with her father's wishes I went about the task of finding her a suitable match with impunity."

Sir Sydney began pacing as he became more agitated. "But...what nonsense...I am head of the family, all decisions regarding matrimony should be mine."

Caroline's eyes met Richard's and she sensed his scrutiny of her. Was he asking for her support?

"That is where you are wrong Sydney," Lady Moreton said, "you may have the title and think of yourself as head of the family, but you do not have the estate or the right to wield power over any family members here present."

Sydney strode across the room to the squire. "As local magistrate, act sir. Act at once, I demand it!"

"And what am I to act upon?" the squire replied. "You say your cousin has been married against her will. She says not. You say you are her guardian, your aunt says not. And although I am not in a position to make any judgement on inheritance, the case seems straightforward. Sir Henry inherited Moreton Arnscote, so did the man make a will? And if so to whom has be bequeathed his lands and possessions?"

Caroline felt all eyes in the room turn on her. She straightened her back and raised her head. "My father left several papers, some of which I have not been through, there is possibly a will amongst them. I recall he did have a meeting with a local attorney a few days before he died. Mr. Hawkins, our local vicar also attended."

"Then where can we find this document?" Squire Talbot asked.

"At Moreton Arnscote," Caroline replied.

The squire nodded and a smile crossed his face. "We must away then, all of us, as soon as we have settled this matter we can have a decent meal and catch up on the sleep we were deprived of last night." He turned to Richard, "Could we trouble you for the use of your carriage. I think it best you travel with me. Sir Sydney, please bring your carriage with your men and Lady Moreton, perhaps you will chaperone your niece."

Richard disliked travelling by carriage at the best of times but especially today. However, he had given his word to the squire not to act foolishly. By doing so it meant he had to tolerate the gentleman's company for the journey. He would have preferred to ride, or at least drive himself. Then he would be able to indulge his thoughts, clear his head of the chaos Moreton had created by his unexpected invasion of his privacy and his house the previous night. However, he had no doubt in his mind that this ridiculous matter of the inheritance would be settled quickly once Caroline had located her father's will. He sincerely hoped she had one of the originals. That would solve the question finally. But, if she hadn't preserved her father's papers adequately, he might have to play his ace card. He already had a copy of Sir Henry's will.

The fact that he had already obtained a copy from Mr. Hawkins, duly signed and witnessed as authentic put his mind at ease. Unless he had to produce the document and explain how it came to be in his possession.

What would Caroline think of him then? What did she think of him now? He wished he could speak to her and assure her of his most earnest intentions. But would that be enough? Undoubtedly she would question his motives for calling upon Mr. Hawkins before he made contact with her. Why hadn't he been able to explain her true position in the Moreton family to her at that first meeting then none of his misunderstanding would have come about. *But mother would have none of it.* He reminded himself.

"Splendid day, eh colonel?" Squire Talbot said as he looked out of the window. "I'm hoping for a better harvest this year, after the dreadful weather we have had for the past three seasons. Need less rain, my grain went mouldy on the stalks, last year."

Richard nodded his agreement but the very last topic on which he wanted to converse was agriculture. He knew his own estate lacked the care and husbandry of either Squire Talbot's or Moreton Arnscote, but he didn't have the blunt of either of those estates. True, the Moreton share was by far the largest, indeed, during the short time he had been managing the land despite the poor harvests, the returns had been five times his own. But when the yields of the plantations in the West Indies had been added to the total income, Moreton Arnscote was worth ten thousand a year. And he had kept that vital intelligence from Caroline. The matter weighed heavily upon his shoulders and he had no idea how he might put it right.

"Regret how you were treated last night," the squire said, "but when Sir Sydney turned up with his heavies, I had to act as he was on his way to the Grange whether I accompanied him or not. As to where he hired those ruffians from, I have no idea. They are certainly not locals."

"Moreton has enemies in London, he rarely goes out alone for fear of his life. I know that he has lived these two years past on the promise of his inheritance. Now that appears to be slipping out of his grasp, we must all take great care, especially Caroline."

"And yourself, colonel, do not forget if Sir Sydney ever hopes to claim the estate then he must do so over your dead body, and your wife's, of course."

"Do not worry about me, squire, I can look after myself."

"I'm not doubting that, sir, but desperate men can do desperate things and I can't see Moreton lying down with his legs in the air."

"Can't bring yourself to call him Sir Sydney, eh?"

Richard watched the squire's piggy eyes narrow. What was he really asking? The squire must know there was no friendship between them, although they had been acquainted in boyhood and been required to play together when Sydney visited his uncle and aunt. But childhood acquaintance does not merit life-long loyalty unless there was a bond of friendship.

Whilst Richard maintained polite conversation with the squire his thoughts kept drifting back to Caroline. Her image flashed before him whenever he closed his eyelids, he remembered the softness of her skin and sweet smell of her body. The more he thought of her, the more he wanted her. But now she was beyond his reach, albeit only temporarily, at least that is what he hoped. He closed his eyes and thought of her, how he should have been waking up this morning and making love to her exquisite body, instead he had spent a sleepless night tied to a chair. And today? Instead of exploring her delicate secret places he was bumping along in a carriage with only a bumbling country squire for company. He let out a long sigh and asked the question he knew would enable the squire to ramble for several minutes. "Have your ewes produced well?"

Caroline sat opposite her aunt in the Moreton carriage and waited for her to speak. They had parted at their previous meeting earlier that morning not on the best of terms and she was sure Lady Moreton would bear grudges long after most people had forgiven and forgotten. There were so many questions she wanted to ask. However, when it was revealed her father had requested Lady Moreton to become her guardian her situation changed. She thought for a few moments, glancing occasionally at her aunt. It was time to ask for the truth. "There have been several matter puzzling me since I arrived at Moreton Arnscote."

"Really? Then perhaps I can help." Lady Moreton smiled serenely, which immediately placed Caroline on her guard.

"Why didn't you tell me you were my guardian?"

"My dear, I thought you already knew. Didn't your father inform you he had written to me?"

"He did not. He asked me to send his letter when he had passed on and did not make me party to the contents. I admit I was sorely tempted to open it. However, I felt bound to carry out his wishes."

"Most commendable, my dear, but regardless of Sir Sydney's threats, I have your father's letter placing you in my guardianship. Sir Henry specifically requested me to help find you a suitable husband, which I have done. And now, because of your cousin's interference, our family will be the laughing stock of the Season. I doubt if any of us, except Sydney, will be able to show our faces in London again."

Caroline raised her eyebrows, a London Season was far from her mind if not totally absent. Should she admit she had only accepted her aunt's invitation in the hope of assistance in securing a suitable governess position? Instead her aunt had found her a husband. There seemed little point so she dismissed the idea. "My next question is a delicate matter as I assumed Moreton Arnscote belonged to you, or possibly Richard. This whole business is about the estate, isn't it?"

Lady Moreton stiffened. "Yes, but I do not like discussing monetary matters. It is vulgar for a lady to do so. You would be wise to learn from my instruction and let men handle business affairs."

Her aunt's answer felt like a reprimand but Caroline was in no mood to argue. Silently she realised her life, happiness and future might depend on the outcome of a single document her father might have signed on his deathbed. If her understanding was correct, and she had no reason to doubt the rationale of her thinking, and her father had left all his property and worldly goods to his only daughter, then Moreton Arnscote was hers. But aged eighteen, a minor in the eyes of the law, could she still inherit or would the estate fall into the hands of her guardian? Sir Sydney's interest in her became acutely apparent, but then so did Richard's. He had married her, willingly taken her to his bed, given her his name but would he ever love her?

Or was marriage merely the channel through which he planned to satisfy his avarice? A path supported wholeheartedly by his mother.

The carriage rattled over an uneven part of the road as the driver turned the horses and they passed through the gates of Moreton Arnscote.

From inside the bedchamber Caroline had occupied during her brief stay on the estate, she summoned her maid. "Where has my father's sea chest been stored?"

"I placed it at the foot of this cupboard," Brown replied and pointed to the corner of the room. "Shall I bring it out ma'am?"

"Place it on top of the ottoman," Caroline said but when she saw the girl struggle with the heavy trunk she helped her lift it up. Opening the lid, she found the red and gold gown Lady Moreton had lent her for the wedding.

Brown's cheeks pinked. "I'm sorry miss, I mean ma'am, but I didn't know what to do with the gown once you had changed. I couldn't leave it on the bed, so I put it in here with your special things. I hope I did right ma'am, but there was no one to ask as we were all off to Weston Grange."

Caroline picked up the heavy garment, her fingers caressing the ruby red silk heavily embroidered with gold thread. "It is a magnificent gown, but I prefer the more modern fashions." She placed the gown over her arm and carried it to the bed where she laid it down.

Returning to the chest, she picked up the first bunch of documents, untied the ribbon securing them and began sifting through each one. The bundle only contained records of her father's sea voyages and annual accounts dating back several years. She placed them neatly in a pile once she had glanced over them. "Re-tie that bundle," she instructed the maid.

There was a knock on the door which Brown answered. It was the butler, who stepped into the room. "Mrs. Weston, Squire Talbot wishes to know if you have found the document."

Caroline looked across the room at him. "I am still searching. When I have found it I shall come down. Where is he waiting?"

"In the library ma'am with Lady Moreton,

Colonel Weston and Sir Sydney Moreton," he replied.

"And those two men accompanying Sir Sydney are they still with him?"

"They have been persuaded to eat in the servants' hall and are devouring large quantities of cold meat and ale left from yesterday's festivities."

"I hope they continue to remain there for I find their presence very intimidating."

"Yes, ma'am, I will endeavour to keep them occupied for as long as possible." He gave a slight bow and left.

Caroline continued with her task until she opened the third bundle. "Got it!" she cried and waved her father's will in the air. Then it occurred to her to check the signatures and the date. It was indeed her father's hand, plus that of Mr. Hawkins, the local clergyman and Dr. Evans who had attended her father during his last days.

Will in hand, she descended the stairs.

Richard sat in a corner of the library. He had not spoken more than a few words to his mother other than to rise when she entered the room with Sir Henry's letter in her hand.

"Look, look," she had insisted, "there he writes to Sir William and asks that '*you and your good lady take my beloved daughter, Caroline, into your household, please care for her as if she were your own and assist in finding her a suitable husband.*'"

Squire Talbot had requested to see the letter and Sir Sydney had paced around the room like a disgruntled cockerel. So Richard had resumed his seat when his mother had sat down.

He felt guilty because he knew the contents of Sir Henry's will and had obtained a copy from the good vicar at Lee Cove. So for him there would be no revelation of the truth when Caroline finally appeared. He felt a wretchedness of mind, previous unknown to him as he would have to act as though he knew nothing. Deceiving Caroline was cutting him to the quick.

Would his mother have treated Caroline so kindly had she already been married? He doubted it. He was very familiar with his mother's manipulative nature having witnessed her twist Sir William around her little finger whenever the fancy took her. And now he had allowed her to manipulate him, why?

The answer was simple, money. Weston Grange needed finance to rebuild the farm cottages, refurbish the house, provide the wherewithal to continue his stud and provide him with a comfortable living. He had decided to marry several months before his mother had produced 'the answer to my prayers', as she had secretly dubbed Caroline. His bride needed to be an heiress, preferably at least tolerable, but certainly one with the blunt. And yet as he waited for Caroline to appear to announce her good news, he could not throw off the melancholies brought about by guilt.

Had she realised her true financial worth? She would be a fool if she had not done so already, and he knew she was no fool. And what of their marriage?

Sydney could not have arrived at a more timely moment. Indeed it was almost melodramatic and could not have been scripted better if the scene belonged in a comedy play. The villain arrives to discover the hero and heroine in the same bed. The marriage act is interrupted and the heroine is still a virgin. He closed his eyes and hoped his bride would refrain from imparting the non-consummation fact to either Squire Talbot or her cousin Sydney.

He folded his arms and dropped his head into his chest. Memories of those few brief moments he had shared in bed with her kept invading his senses. Her softness, her perfume, the taste of her skin, the sensations her body had created from the merest touch of skin on skin, they engulfed him and allowed his true feelings to emerge to betray him. He wanted her, physically, mentally, emotionally....in every way. Could he be falling in love with her?

Caroline rushed into the library. "I have found it," she declared holding the sheet of paper up for all to see and feeling a lurch of excitement surge through her.

"May I see it?" the squire asked.

She handed it to him and scanned the room. She had been so excited when she entered she hadn't been aware of exactly who was present. Lady Moreton sat near to the fire screen in front of the hearth although on a warm spring day no fire had been lit. Squire Talbot paced the carpet in the centre of the room as he read the document. Sir Sydney took a few paces towards her, she thought he was about to speak as his mouth took on an unpleasant twist. She wanted to ask him about the guardianship he had laid claim to but decided to wait until the subject was raised either by him or another. But where was Richard?

She looked over her shoulder and found him leaning against shelves of books behind the door. No wonder she hadn't seen him when she stepped into the room. He met her eyes and a bland half smile creased the right side of his face. But even a slight smile from him was sufficient to send heat flowing through her veins.

Fearing she was blushing, she crossed the room and sat near to her aunt, who also gave her a smile. To Caroline, the sincerity of Lady Moreton's expression was moot but propriety prevented her from questioning her.

"This seems to be in order," the squire said. "There is no probate court stamp or date. Has this will been proven?"

Fear knotted inside Caroline as her heart beat quickened. She felt momentary panic as her mind raced towards a vague and shadowy future. But knowing she had to conceal her inner feelings, she took a deep breath and hoped when she spoke her voice would be calm and steady. She glanced at Lady Moreton, then over her shoulder at Richard hoping for some kind of moral support. The magnetism of his smile strengthened her to speak the truth.

"No, sir, it has not. There were some pressing business matters to be settled and I had no notion my father had inherited title, land or property. After settling his funeral expenses, I was seeking a position as a governess when I received my aunt's invitation."

"Not proven!" Sir Sydney declared striding

across the room. He grabbed the will from Squire Talbot. "This isn't worth the paper it's written upon!" He screwed it up in his hands and flung it at the fireplace. It bounced off the fire screen onto the carpet close to Caroline's foot.

She retrieved it and began straightening it out.

"Moreton," Richard called and emerged from his corner, "that was most foolish. I know you hold any barrier to you inheriting the estate in contempt but go against Sir Henry's will at your peril. I shall accompany my wife to Lichfield this afternoon where we shall lodge Sir Henry's will at the Probate Court."

"Upon whose authority?" Sir Sydney cried. "Who is named as the executor, surely, he had the good sense to name a family member?"

"Why it is Miss Caroline Moreton...but she is a minor," Squire Talbot said.

"That is why I shall be accompanying her," Richard replied.

"This is preposterous," Sir Sydney declared, "Sir Henry did not live in the neighbourhood, his will should be proven either in the West country or London."

"No sir," the squire said emphatically, "wills can be proven at any probate court in England and Wales. I have that on the best advice." He turned to Richard, "Go at once colonel, I believe you haven't a minute to lose."

"Indeed sir, I shall take your excellent advice." Richard turned to Sir Sydney, "As for you Moreton, take yourself and your two henchmen and leave my wife's estate."

Sir Sydney's eyes narrowed. "Are you

threatening me Weston?"

"If that is what you wish to believe," Richard replied.

"Then take care Weston." He turned to Caroline, "Wife indeed, cousin? I wish you happy, if you can be in the knowledge that your husband married you for your money."

Caroline's mouth dropped open, she wanted to speak but could not form her words. A sharp pain stabbed her chest as his words *married you for your money* became etched upon her heart.

"How dare you insult my wife in her own house, be gone sir, be gone from this place at once and do not cross either my wife's threshold or mine ever again."

Sir Sydney stared coldly first at Richard, then at Caroline. His face coloured a deep shade of puce. He turned sharply and addressed the butler who was waiting at the door. "Send to the stables for my carriage and notify my men we are leaving." He turned his back on his family and left without another word.

CHAPTER EIGHT

Despite his dislike of carriage travel, Richard sat inside next to Caroline as they set off along the Stafford road. Lady Moreton had asked if he wished her to accompany them. But he had refused. He wanted time alone with his wife, although the journey shouldn't take more than an hour and a half to cover the twelve miles to the cathedral city of Lichfield and the probate court.

However, it was noon when they set out and with no idea how long the court declarations would take, or even if they would be able to lodge the will that day, Richard ordered a second carriage to follow them with Caroline's maidservant, his valet and provisions for an overnight stop possibly at the George in Lichfield. Not only did he ensure their coachman had an armed guard accompanying his carriage but also, the servants' coach was similarly guarded.

He did not trust Sydney. The indignation he had suffered by the crass disturbance of his wedding night would have been sufficient to call the man out. But Sydney would never face him in a fair fight. The man had been a liar and a cheat as a boy and he doubted if his step-cousin's character had been reformed by the idle life he lived in London.

"We may have to stay overnight in Lichfield," Richard said, "I hope you don't mind." He moved his thigh closer to hers as he spoke. She seemed to flinch as she started to adjust the bow of her bonnet, busying her hands. He had hoped to take one of them in his. *No matter,* he thought, *I must not force myself upon her.*

The notion that his action might be construed as such caused him to draw back. He had never forced himself upon a woman in his life and had no intention of beginning now. But Caroline was different. He had tasted the softness of her delicate skin next to his, had felt the warm of her lips and fondled her firm breasts. He had not known so close proximity with a woman before that he had not made love to. The mere thought of last night tantalised his emotions, such a beautiful prize had been dangled before him, a few more moments in their marital bed and he would have taken her virginity. More importantly he believed she would have given it willingly. But now?

"Did Sir Sydney's ruffians treat you ill last night?" she asked.

He was almost grateful for the question but didn't want to alarm her with his reply. He shook his head. "My annoyance at being parted from you outweighed any pain I might have suffered."

"But those men treated you most brutally, punching you in the stomach and groin. I thought some great catastrophe had occurred or the house was ablaze at the very least," she said.

"Thank you for your concern, my dear, time

cures most wounds. Squire Talbot acted bravely in my defence and insisted I was restrained in my own bedchamber but Sydney refused to call off his henchmen, so I spent an uncomfortable night tied in a chair, not the best place for sleep. It reminded me of the Peninsular. I swear after a few weeks on the road with the army, it is possible to sleep anywhere and at anytime."

"And at Waterloo?"

He did not reply immediately. A knot seemed to catch in his throat preventing him from speaking. It was at those odd moments, when he thought he had left all the tell-tale signs of battle behind him that a word or reference to 1815 occurred and caught him unawares. The sound of cannon blasted in his ear, the pounding of horse as the cavalry advanced and always the image of Charles at his side. "Yes," he uttered, "but I do not wish to discuss it."

As they crossed the forested land of Cannock Chase and descended to a small bridge over the river, they met other traffic and their carriage slowed.

Caroline had mulled over his swift dismissal of the great battle with some thought. Knowing the way her father had related his experiences of the great naval battle of 1805, Richard's reluctance to indulge himself in the army's great victory over the French surprised her.

Eventually she asked, "Is it much further to Lichfield?"

Richard, who had been looking out of the open

window, glanced back over his shoulder and captured her eyes with his grey ones. Usually thought provoking and probing, now they were tender. "We shall pass through a small market town called Rugeley, change horses before we climb up Brereton hill, then we should be able to see the spires of Lichfield cathedral. We have about six miles to go." He tore his gaze away from her, settled back into the corner of the carriage and stretched out his long limbs.

She gave him a sideways glance, thought about turning to face him, but saw he was looking out of the window. His face in profile would have made an excellent cameo like the ones she had seen at the rectory where she stayed for a few months after her mother died. She smiled inwardly as the memory of those days came flooding back. How surprised she had been that the rector and his wife spoke English at home, whereas she had spoken only French. In her childhood naivety she had thought English was for church and French for home. As there were no other children at the rectory, Mrs Hawkins taught her sewing, drawing, reading and how to play the pianoforte, whilst instructing her to read and write in both languages.

Thus as a small child of seven her days were filled with new things which helped her cope with the loss of her mother, indeed Mrs Hawkins had become her second mother.

When the captain returned home for good, he allowed the lessons to continue and Mrs Hawkins became not only Caroline's mentor but also her confidante. *If only Mrs Hawkins had been alive to help and comfort me when father lingered between life and death,*" she thought. "If only," she said aloud without meaning to be heard.

"If only what?" Richard asked turning back to her.

"Oh, it is nought," she replied.

"Nought, but something's playing on your mind. Were you disappointed by the wedding night?"

His direct question surprised her, what could she say? What was the truth? "Everything has happened so quickly, I can scarce get my bearings."

"I agree, rushing to lodge a will in probate is hardly how I would have expected to spend our honeymoon, however, if we are kept waiting at the court, or indeed if it is not open today, then we shall overnight at the George. It is a fine establishment of good repute, I am sure we shall get good victuals there and a comfortable bed."

She felt a hot flush pink her cheeks when he made reference to a bed. The memory of their closeness the previous night was so firmly fixed in her mind that had they not been so rudely disturbed what other secrets of the human anatomy might she have discovered?

The carriage rattled along the road and began a slow descent into the Vale of Lichfield. However, the sun went in and dark clouds gathered. "There could be a rain shower before we arrive," he said, "but we can't let the weather get in the way of business, can we my dearest?" He picked up her gloved hand in his, brought it to his lips and very gently kissed her fingertips.

A tingling sensation ran down the length of her arm. And although her hand was gloved, his action hinted at a closer intimacy between them. She squeezed her left-hand fingers together so she could feel the hard gold wedding band he had placed on her third finger the previous day.

The carriage rolled along the Stafford road and entered Lichfield from the north. Caroline leaned out of the window as they passed carts loaded with farm produce on their way to market, drays loaded with barrels and livestock being driven. It seemed everyone was going in the same direction towards the three elegant spires rising majestically over the town.

"If we have time to spare," Richard said, "we must visit the cathedral. Although it does not rival York or Canterbury for size, it is a remarkable building and well-worth internal inspection."

She abandoned her window view and sank back into the corner of the well-padded seat. "I shall look forward to it but where is the probate court located?"

His mouth broadened into a smile. "Do I detect a sense of urgency in your desire to claim your inheritance?" he said in a teasing tone.

"I would prefer this matter to be settled with all expediency, but as to my inheritance, will it be possible to take legal advice whilst we are here?"

He nodded. "I was about to suggest that course of action, for not only do we have the question of your inheritance but also that of the legal standing of our wedding."

She pressed her lips together. She had not expected him to be so direct but had to admit the matter weighed heavily on her mind. If the will was proven and if she became the legal owner of Moreton Arnscote, would it be hers? Or would it be placed in the hands of her legal guardian until she reached her majority? But moreover, who was her legal guardian if the marriage was valid?

Unable to hold her tongue any longer, she struggled to keep all expression from her voice when she asked, "If our wedding is legal, then you will inherit all my property and worldly goods, won't you?"

He raised his eyebrows. "Yes, my dear Caro, that is the law."

"But there has been no settlement agreed between us regarding my financial position."

"Again, that is so, but would you rather have your dear cousin negotiate on your behalf, for I very much doubt he would make any agreement that would benefit you or your offspring."

At the mention of children she felt her cheeks flame. "No, Sir Sydney appears a bombastic individual who favours his own person. He bears grievance that he is not to inherit and I fear his resentment might cause trouble."

"Hmm," he nodded. "Your acute appraisal of his character is most exacting, I must ask you one day what is your opinion of mine? However, please let us not deviate from our purpose today. We shall soon be stopping at the George, where they will attend to the horses and I will engage rooms."

"Are we to remain the night?"

"Only if it is necessary, however, I doubt if there will be sufficient light for us to embark upon our return journey today."

Although he had mentioned that they might overnight in Lichfield, the thought of spending it in an inn with him as husband and wife had not really occurred to her. She recalled the several nights they had spent at inns along the road from Devon when he had collected her from Lee Cove. She had slept alone in her bed with a maid in the room but tonight might be different. Would he expect to spend the night in her bed?

They waited a short while outside the office of the probate court attached to the cathedral before they were called inside. Richard explained their business to the clerk and produced the documents.

The clerk read the will through carefully before looking up at them. "This appears to be in order," he said. "Are you Miss Catherine Moreton?"

"Yes, you have my father's will before you."

"And do you have any proof that you are that person, or any documents, letters of recommendation from the witnesses to this will?"

"I...no I don't"

"Perhaps these letters will confirm Miss Moreton's identity," Richard said and handed the clerk a small bundle of letters.

A wave of apprehension swept though her and she looked at Richard quizzically. What documents was he offering to the court official? He had said nothing previously. Her heartbeat quickened, he undoubtedly knew more about her than she had realised and when the clerk asked if the Rev. Mr. Hawkins was the same gentleman who had witnessed the will, she was left in no doubt of her suspicions. She wanted Richard to explain his involvement in her affairs, but this was no place to start asking questions.

The clerk agreed to accept the documents, wrote out a receipt describing what had been deposited with him and tied all the papers together with red tape.

"How long will the will take to prove?" Richard asked. "You are fortunate, the court sits on the morrow and there is only one other case," the clerk replied as he handed the receipt to Richard. Emerging from the probate office, Caroline took the arm Richard offered her. "If we walk around the cathedral close we can call at the offices of Mr. Brimstow. It may be fortuitous to acquaint him with what we have done as he holds documents relating to Moreton Arnscote."

"Who is he?" she asked, feeling slightly overwhelmed by the speed their business had been conducted.

Richard placed his right hand over hers and squeezed gently. "An attorney who has been dealing with the late Sir William's affairs, indeed, he has spent considerable time trying to establish the whereabouts of your father for nearly two years." Her nerves tensed and she came to an abrupt stop. "This is a strange matter surely my father could have been easily located from the navy list?"

He half turned to face her. "Yes, one would have thought so, however, it did not prove to be the situation. For some reason, possibly only known to himself, your father was not listed after Trafalgar."

Caroline shivered.

"Are you cold?" he asked.

"No," she shook her head. In truth she felt as if a hand had closed around her throat. Anxious to divert his attention from her inner emotions she looked up to the sky at the dark clouds gathering. "The temperature has fallen, it looks like rainfall is imminent. Perhaps we should hurry. Is it far to Mr. Brimstow's?" She felt his grip on her hand squeeze tighter as they rounded the corner into Dam Street where he halted abruptly. He turned towards her and placed his hands around her shoulders. "What's the matter?" she asked as he pressed her against the wall.

"I've just spotted Sydney coming out of Brimstow's chambers."

Warning spasms coursed through her. "Is he coming this way?"

"Fortunately not, he is walking towards the market square."

Swallowing the fear that had caught in her throat, she looked up. "What can this mean? Does he have business affairs with Brimstow too?"

"I don't know." His voice was soothing yet oddly disconcerting. "We shall have to see what Brimstow has to say, if ought. I can only surmise your cousin has called upon the attorney in respect to the estate. But knowing Sydney, I wouldn't put any form of skullduggery beyond him. He has disappeared from view, so come, we must make our mark with the lawyer."

They entered a tall three storey house via the central doorway that opened directly onto the street and waited in the stone-flagged hallway. A small man with a slight stoop greeted them and asked their business.

"Taylor, don't you recognise me, Colonel Richard Weston? I would be obliged to see Mr. Bristow."

"Ah, so it is you Colonel, 'though I scarce recognised you out of uniform. Why it must be some while since we saw you here. I will inform Mr. Bristow you are waiting upon him. Would you and the lady prefer to avail yourselves of our drawing room?"

Without asking her opinion, Richard said, "Of course, come my dear," and he indicated the door on the left-hand side of the hall.

When they were inside, Taylor said, "If you will excuse me, sir, I will inform Mr. Bristow you are waiting upon him."

Caroline sat down by the fireplace and Richard took the seat on the opposite side. She glanced around the panelled room which seemed rather dark, despite the two sash windows looking out onto the street. The ease with which the depositing of her father's will for probate had surprised her for she believed the whole process would be a more lengthy one and was about to remark upon it when the door opened and a grey middle-aged man entered.

"My dear Colonel how pleased I am to see you again and looking in good health." He peered over gold-rimmed spectacles as he advanced across the room and shook Richard's hand heartily.

Towering over the man, for he had arisen when Bristow entered, Richard beamed back at him.

The cheerfulness expressed in Richard's face quite took her breath away. She felt her heart skip. She opened her mouth to speak but realised she had not been introduced and that is when her heart sank. How would Richard describe her?

"Bristow, we have several matters requiring your advice, may we discuss these in the privacy of your office?" Richard asked.

"Of course, please come this way." He gave Caroline a singular glance and led the way across the hall to the opposite door.

So, I am not to be introduced as neither Miss Moreton nor Mrs Weston she thought and felt a little piqued by both Richard's and Mr. Bristow's apparent lack of manners. However, she followed them into the office, a room of not dissimilar proportions to the one they had just quitted. It also faced the street but the lower half of the windows were shuttered and Bristow had candles despite it being the mid-afternoon.

He took the seat behind a large heavy mahogany desk and indicated two seats on the other side for them.

Richard turned to her and held the chair as she sat down. Only when they were both seated did Bristow sit down.

"Now Colonel what is so pressing?" he asked.

"Mr. Bristow," Richard began, "there are two matters, both connected, that have brought us here with all haste today." He told him about depositing Sir Henry's will at the probate court. Bristow clenched his hands together as he listened to the account, nodding his agreement as Richard described the documents he had also left with the probate court clerk. They included copies of signed statements from Rev. Mr. Hawkins of Lee Cove, and certified copies of parish register entries for her father and mother's marriage and her baptism.

The extent of the documentation surprised her. Where had Richard obtained all this information and so quickly? She wanted to ask him but decided such enquiry would best be made in private.

"You have been most efficient," Bristow said, "and I assume the case will be heard tomorrow."

"Yes," Richard nodded.

Then Bristow turned to her. "Can I assume you are Miss Moreton, Sir Henry Moreton's daughter and sole heir?"

Caroline gulped she had not expected the attorney to be so direct. She nodded then gaining her voice said, "Yesterday the colonel and I were married but my cousin, Sir Sydney Moreton insists we are not as I have not yet reached my majority and did not have his permission to marry. I am confused, Mr. Bristow, and wish to know how the law is interpreted in my case."

Bristow raised his eyebrows, "Of course you do. Now let me ask a few questions regarding the marriage which I hope you will be able to answer truthfully."

"Were you married in the Church of England by an ordained minister thereof?"

"Yes," Richard replied, "by special licence provided by the bishop."

"And did you at the time of the marriage have a legal guardian? By legal I mean one appointed by your father or mother in their stead."

This time Richard did not answer but gave her

a penetration gaze. She felt the strength of his clear grey eyes boring into her. What did he expect her to say? Had the attorney not asked her to answer truthfully?

"I understand my father requested his brother, Sir William Moreton and his wife Lady Moreton to look after me. So I suppose my aunt, Lady Moreton is my guardian, but I was not aware of the fact when I agreed to marry the colonel."

"I see, but that does not alter the fact that Lady Moreton was given the position by your father and that she accepted it." Bristow glanced quickly between them.

"Did you enter upon the marriage of your own free will?" he asked her.

Caroline thought for a few moments, there had been other circumstances, but what could she say? That the colonel had blackmailed her? That she had tried to run away from him and placed herself in a precarious position which could have ruined her reputation? She glanced quickly at Richard who was looking away, so she could not catch his eye. "Yes, I married freely," she said softly.

Richard looked back at her. His expression had softened. With relief she wondered, but again she could hardly ask him in front of Bristow.

"My final question is only intended to clarify the situation and possible consequences or legal paths that might be taken. Colonel, I put this question to you first, has the marriage been consummated?"

Richard straightened his back. "No sir, it has not. We were disturbed in the marital bed by Squire Talbot and Sir Sydney brandishing two pistols. I was restrained by Sir Sydney's henchmen until this morning."

Caroline felt her fingers tingling and grasped her gloved hands together, her muscles tightened as she waited for Bristow to explain their legal situation. He shook his head and she thought he was about to say that she was indeed subject to her cousin's whim, that the marriage yesterday had been illegal and what of her reputation?

"Your marriage is legal, you are indeed Mrs Weston. Whether the marriage is consummated is a matter between husband and wife, with regard to the law you have gone through a legal ceremony witnessed by many and 'what God have joined in holy matrimony, let no man put asunder'. However, as the marriage has not been consummated it is legally possible to annul it, if both parties agree. This is a matter for the Church Court and such cases do take some time and are usually only heard when there is some impediment rendering the marriage act impossible to perform. If Sir Sydney had intended to prevent your marriage then he should have arrived earlier at the church before you made your vows. Now, is there anything else with which I may be assistance?" he looked at both of them in turn.

"Could we impose upon you tomorrow? We would greatly appreciate you attendance at the probate court, I believe the case will be heard at eleven?" Richard asked.

"Of course...I will ensure Taylor enters the appointment in my daily book."

Upon taking their leave from Bristow's Dam Street office, Caroline took Richard's arm and they made their way towards the market square where most of the stalls were packing up their wares for the day. The late afternoon sun glinted on the tall steeple of St Mary's church as the clock struck four.

"Perhaps we should retire to the George," Richard suggested, "I have a mighty appetite and would welcome my dinner."

Caroline agreed as she wanted some answers to the many questions buzzing in her head. How had Richard been able to secure so many documents in such a short space of time and would the evidence presented to the probate court be sufficient for her claim on the estate. But then, she was legally married to him, so wouldn't the entire house and lands belong to Richard tomorrow.

The next day seemed far off. They were legally man and wife, so didn't that mean the nuptials so rudely interrupted the previous night could be resumed? As they strolled along Market Street, she couldn't help but notice the many shops selling all manner of goods. There was everything from bales of very fine dress fabric to silversmiths with a wonderful array of highly polished wares adorning their shop windows. Caroline had never seen a more diverse range of goods and would have loved to have stopped but their destination was getting closer.

With the entrance to the stable yard of the hotel before them, Richard turned to her and said, "The hour is growing late, we shall not make Moreton before nightfall. We must take advantage of the rooms I have reserved for us."

Was it the cajoling tone of his voice, the slight emphasis on them taking 'advantage of the rooms' phrase or merely her imagination? She didn't know but her skin prickled pleasurably at the thought of physical contact with him again in the confines of a shared bed. She squeezed her hand and felt the unfamiliar hardness of the gold wedding band on her finger.

Once inside the servants could not have been more helpful and soon she was enjoying the comfort of a small private sitting room sipping tea.

Not long afterwards, hot soup was served, again in the small sitting room, followed by a generous helping of steak pie. Richard ate heartily as he sat across the narrow table. "Best we eat here," he said, "it can become very noisy in the dining room."

"It is not the noise that concerns me but the likelihood of being confronted by Sir Sydney again. What do you think he was doing at Bristow's earlier?"

"Probably consulting him on some matter relating to the estate. Bristows have long represented Moreton since before my step-father's time, possibly even longer."

"But surely Mr. Brimstow cannot be that old?"

"No, my dear," Richard chuckled. "I refer to Brimstow's father, he founded the firm nigh on fifty years ago."

"Oh, I see, how foolish of me." She slipped another piece of the tender steak into her mouth and felt rather naive. There seemed so much to learn and she was grateful he had included her when they visited the probate office, but from the attitude of the probate clerk and to some extent from Brimstow, she gathered the feeling that legal matters were very much a male domain where any female would not be welcome. However, she knew she had to ask Richard some questions and what better time when he appeared relaxed and his appetite satisfied by a hearty meal.

"The documents you presented to the probate court what did they contain?"

Seated across the table from her he hesitated before replying, was he measuring her? His face closed, as if guarding a secret. "Signed statements from the witnesses to your father's will, Rev. Mr. Hawkins signed a copy of the parish record of your baptism and a similar document regarding your father's marriage-"

"But how did you obtain this information in so little time?"

"I had to have evidence regarding your birth to prove your inheritance. I had been in the neighbourhood for several days before I arrived to collect you from Lee Cove. I had already spoken to Mr. Hawkins. He supplied me with written confirmation of your birth, your parents' marriage and a copy of your father's will."

"My father's...will," she stammered. Her fingers tensed and blood pounded in her head as he revealed the extent of his activity. "You knew about the inheritance before you came to collect me. Did you plan the wedding too before you had seen the bride?" Her mind became congested with doubts and fears. "Why did you marry me?"

Slowly he removed his napkin and pushed his chair a few inches away from the table. His chin dropped onto his chest, so she could only see the top of his head, not his face. In the silence that stretched out between them, her stomach churned half in anticipation, half in dread of what his answer might be. Could she trust him?

"I've answered that question before," he replied in a raised tone. He looked up and glowered at her. "My answer is unchanged. I wanted you the first time I saw you at Lee Cove. Whether you choose to believe me rests with you. I will not deny I knew the estate would pass to you. And I know it should have been Charles, believe me I would have moved heaven and earth if I could have saved that boy, but we cannot undo time. My estate is a very poor neighbour to Moreton. I could not contemplate marriage without some attention to money. So, I took every step possible to ensure Moreton Arnscote remained in safe hands."

She felt her neck muscles tighten as she reacted angrily to the challenge in his voice. "And that meant marrying me," she cried.

His expression turned to a rakish sardonic smile but he offered no reply.

She wanted to escape but running away seemed cowardly, she had run away from him before and paid a heavy price for her foolishness. Yet what could she say? He had answered her question with his silence. Slowly and with as much dignity as she could muster she left the room.

Richard watched her walk away. He rose but did not prevent her leaving as she headed for the bedroom which made up their small suite of rooms. Resuming his seat he leaned forward, elbows on the table and cradled his head in his hands. What had he done?

The plan to secure the future of the estate had seemed a deceptively simple one when his mother had outlined it to him.

"If she really is Henry's legal heir, then you must marry her," she had insisted.

"And what if she is already promised or of an intolerable disposition?"

"Richard, sometimes you cause me such vexation! She's a girl, no matter what she looks like, I am confident that with your charms and allurements, you can succeed in this endeavour."

And he had succeeded but at what cost? He had made swift enquiry of the Rev. Mr. Hawkins and made no secret that he represented the Moreton estate when he acquired the necessary documentation to prove her claim. But perhaps it was beneath him to expect her to pay off her father's gambling debts with her virtue. It had been a useful ploy but would he really have taken her virginity under his own roof that day if she had not insisted upon marriage? He honestly didn't know and felt ashamed of himself for being so crass. It was not the behaviour of an officer and a gentleman and at this moment he did not regard himself as either.

What was to be done? Legally they were married and therefore Moreton Arnscote was now, or soon would be, in his hands. His mother's objective had been achieved, although he had no desire to live in the house especially as his mother would hardly be at the point of removal. No, his mind had been made up long before the wedding he would remain in his own establishment, although management of the Moreton estate would be in his hands and therefore secure. But hadn't it been so since he returned from Waterloo and found his step-father devastated mentally by the death of his only son?

Memories of that fateful battle flooded his mind, flashes of gun fire, the acrid smell of cordite, the cries of pain, horses whining, cannon thundering and Charles, his young boyish body sliced almost in two by a cannon ball. He had spared his mother and step-father the final gory details claiming the boy had been shot in the head by a stray musket ball. It had appeared more acceptable to inform them so rather than describe the dreadful sight of his young body ripped nearly in two.

He shook his head, desperately trying to rid his memory of that day. He had to think of the future, but what was the future likely to be?

"Caro...Caro..." he said aloud, "lovely Caro." He suddenly felt weak and vulnerable. He lifted his head, yes of course he wanted her, hadn't he told her so? *I wanted you from the first time I saw you*...indeed it was true, but why hadn't he seen the real reason before? She had looked at him with those rare eyes, proudly she had stood in the desolation of her family home, laid bare of all its previous furnishings and possessions. She had trusted him then and never questioned his motives or that of the family in wanting her to visit the estate and meet her relations. She had fallen easily into their trap, but he didn't want her as his captive because she held the key to the Moreton inheritance. She was special, he'd known it from their first meeting. He forced himself to accept the truth. He wanted her because he had fallen in love with her.

Revelation brought him to his feet. He paced the floor of the small dining parlour, stopped to look through the window at the street below. Raucous sounds from the tavern on the opposite side of the street interspersed with loud laughter filled the evening. He stood and watched a group of men fall into the gutter. One after another they were propelled by the strong arms of the innkeeper or his man. And there they lay in their drunkenness.

Too easy to drown my sorrows in liquor, he told himself. Next door, possibly now abed, lies the woman I have married, the woman I love. How can I win her?

Caroline could have called Brown but dismissed the idea. It was easier to be alone. She struggled with the pins on the front of her dress but gradually managed to free herself from it. Removing her undergarments, she slipped into the nightdress Brown had laid out for her earlier.

One by one she extinguished the candles, leaving only the glowing embers in the small fireplace to light the room. Slowly she turned down the bed covers and climbed between the stiff linen sheets.

She shivered and felt as if ice was forming on her upper arms and shoulders. She rubbed them vigorously. Would every night of her marriage be like this? Heartache almost overwhelmed her as she sank into despair. Would she be abandoned after tomorrow when the court settled probate and ownership of Moreton Arnscote passed to her legal husband? And would he ever be a husband to her? Or would he leave her to dwell with her aunt, or should she refer to her as mother-in-law? And family? If he chose not to visit her bed there would never be any children. That thought left her bereft.

A child? A son to inherit? A daughter to love, nurture and educate in the finer points of womanhood? She drew her knees up to her chest and clasped her arms around her legs. Head resting on her knee caps, she wrapped herself in a cocoon of anguish and sank into the depths of wretchedness. Never before, even when her beloved had father died, had she feel so low.

She had no idea how long she remained so, except when she raised her head and looked around the glow from the hearth had diminished thus clothing the room in darkness. It suited her mood. She rubbed her eyes and found she had been crying.

Why does it have to be so?

It felt like the heat of one small candle burning slowly somewhere inside her. Distant at first but acutely aware of a flame beginning to glimmer – hope? Slowly she allowed her subconscious thoughts to rise to the surface of her reasoning. Their marriage did not have to be so desolate. They had exchanged vows and with that went responsibility. Didn't she as a wife have conjugal rights too?

The question rattled around in her head for

several minutes. What did she really want? She closed her eyes and let her thoughts wander, a comfortable home, a man who would love and support her and children. Moreton Arnscote could be a comfortable home if she was allowed to make it so, Weston Grange would be more of a challenge due to its age and condition but improvements could be made. If she wanted children then she needed a man, preferably her husband so her children could legitimately inherit, so would Richard love and support her?

She knew little of his character, indeed from her brief encounters with him he had proven to be rakish, self-centred and passionate about his horses. But he was decidedly handsome and possibly his offspring would also be so. He may have married her for the estate, but hadn't he said he wanted her from their first meeting?

Would he want me now?

The question was powerful enough to cause the small light of desire within her to burst into flame. Her whole being seemed to be filling with wanting. Was he still in the next room?

Unable to control her curiosity she threw back the covers and tip-toed towards the communicating door. Pressing her ear to the heavy oak panelling, she could hear nothing from within. Slowly, as to make as little noise as possible, she lifted the latch and opened the door a few inches. All was darkness within, except the flickering of the fire. Sliding through the gap she advanced a few steps into the parlour. Richard was still there, sitting in the chair, his large frame slumped forwards over the table, his head resting on his forearms. She stared longingly at him. He appeared so attractive even in sleep. A sense of urgency drove her, there was unfinished business between them and she was determined to see it through before sunrise.

She moved to his side and reached out to him running her fingers over his shoulder. He began to stir and she quickly withdrew her hand as if she had been scorched by the heat emanating from him. But he did not awaken.

She leant closer to him, almost brushing his thigh with hers and touched him again. This time she fingered the soft hair at the nape of his neck and couldn't resist sliding her hand down his back when she realised he had loosen his cravat. His skin felt slick to her touch, and as she became extremely conscious of his virile appeal her body began to ache for more. It was like touching forbidden fruit, yet what she was doing wasn't prohibited or beyond the bounds of decorum. She was his wife.

He jolted his head and she stepped back, but not far enough, swift hands encircled her waist and drew her towards him. His gaze bore into her silent expectation. His questioning eyes, bold and seductive, slid downwards and dropped from her face to her shoulders and halted at her breasts only thinly covered by the cotton of her nightgown.

She felt her nipples tighten and begin to tingle. Gently she placed her hand under his chin and raised his head. As she gazed into his eyes, her heart began to race. "You said you wanted me from our first meeting, do you want me now?"

"My love, always." He pushed back his chair and pulled her down onto his lap, his hand slipped to the nape of her neck and gently he drew her towards him. His initial kiss felt soft and tentative, then as the pressure and sensation increased his lips became urgent and demanding, his tongue seeking the softness of her inner palette.

She was in his arms, their bodies pressed together, all barriers between them lifted. She yielded her mouth to him, her arms embraced his powerful shoulders as enticing sensations began to build within her. In the gathering momentum, she did not think of the future. It mattered little, it would wait for tomorrow. Her need for him was similar to those few stolen moments in the library and later outside in the grounds when he had pulled her from behind a tree. But this time was different, this time he had said he wanted her, this time they were husband and wife and this time she finally admitted she wanted him.

"I want a night with you to remember forever," she said, "as last night should have been until we were interrupted."

He swept her up into his arms, stood up and carried her back into the bed chamber and set her down on the bed. As he sat beside her a rakish smile creased his face. "Are you sure this is what you want?"

His question surprised her. Was he about to turn her down? He wouldn't, would he? She took a deep breath. This might be her only chance. "There is nothing I would like more at this moment than to be your wife."

He kissed her again, a strong, passionate and reassuring kiss that sent powerful tingling sensations through to her fingers and toes. She reached for the edge of his waistcoat and eased it off his shoulders. He wriggled out of it and pulled his shirt out of his breeches. Slipping her hand beneath his shirt she felt she was embarking upon a wonderful journey of exploration of male flesh.

With one hand he yanked the garment over his head, cast it aside and wrapped his arms around her. Enthralled she marvelled at the wiry male body hair on his chest as she pressed her head against him and tantalisingly rubbed the palm of her hand over his taut stomach.

His muscles tightened in reaction to her and his mouth sought hers for yet another kiss.

Releasing her, one by one he untied the ribbons down the front of her nightgown to reveal her flesh. He cupped one breast in his hand, pulled her towards him and sank his head to her chest, pushing back the fabric he took her nipple tenderly and licked the burgeoning tip.

She moaned with exquisite delight and he went in search of its twin.

Nurtured and safe in his arms, a growing passion welled up within her. It started in the pit of her stomach and passed unhindered through her nerves and veins, as if the very life blood within was being warmed and nourished by him. Her arousal began deep inside her most feminine parts and began creating a need, which, as yet, she could not fully understand.

"You are absolutely sure about this?" he asked.

"Richard I couldn't be more certain. I want you and that's all that matters to me now."

"And tomorrow?"

"We'll always have today," she breathed

slowly. "None of us know what tomorrow might bring. I want this night, our wedding night, to remember forever." She drew him towards her, felt his warmth and his arousal. Without taking her eyes from his, she skimmed his muscular chest with her palms and brushed his nipples. Then easing her arms from her nightgown, she let it drop to her waist. "I've not done this before," she whispered.

"I wouldn't have expected it," he said, "that's why your first time should be special."

"Then I trust you will make it so, my darling husband."

CHAPTER NINE

Caroline had no idea what time it was when she woke the next morning. The sunlight streamed into her bed chamber and outside in the street she could hear the whine of horses pulling carts and the shouts of traders. She was alone, but the evidence of their night of passion surrounded her. She searched for her discarded nightgown, leapt from the bed to retrieve it and slipped it over her head. Then as she touched the feminine part of her body, she remembered the exquisite pleasure their love-making had given her and a wide smile of satisfaction spread across her face.

Richard had been gentle yet strong. Was he aware of the sheer joy he had given her? She shook her head in amazement at the various feelings lying with a man can bring. She had expected to feel wanted, cherished and warmed but she had not anticipated the explosion of pleasure that the union between man and woman brought.

At one point she had felt very wanton and began to worry that he might think she had not told him the entire truth. But he had encouraged her to let go of her feelings, to relax and enjoy the sensation, and most of all, he had brought her to the peak of her pleasure before enjoying the power of his release. Yet he had not spoken of love.

She sat down on the edge of the bed, only to find the inner parts of her thighs ached from the exertion of the night's activity. Blushing with embarrassment, she climbed under the covers and picked up the small brass bell from the adjacent table and rang it.

"Good morning, ma'am," Brown said as she entered the room. "The colonel said you were not to be disturbed, I hope you have slept well. I can bring you some breakfast from the kitchen if you wish."

"No, I prefer to dress. Where is the colonel?"

"He's gone out, but left instruction that he would return by noon."

"And what time is it now?"

"After ten, ma'am."

"Then we have no time to lose, I'll wear the blue gown and the dark blue pelisse."

Caroline was dressed and finishing a welcoming dish of tea when Richard entered the parlour. Her stomach clenched as she eyed him carefully. He looked handsome in his dark green coat, buff pantaloons and polished Hessians, so dashingly attractive she felt a warm glow flow through her. Satisfaction pursed her lips and she hoped he found her as equally appealing.

"We have an appointment at the Probate Court," he said and offered her his arm.

She took it and together they walked the short distance down the street to the offices at the side of the cathedral where they had called the previous day.

Bristow awaited them as they crossed the threshold. "Good day to your Colonel and Mrs. Weston" he said. "I have had sight of the court documents you lodged yesterday and I don't believe there will be any impediment, of course, the whole case will have to pass through Chancery as the case is already there."

A delay was not what Caroline had expected, but when she thought about the question of Probate, she had no guide to measure the waiting period against. Perhaps she would have to be more patient where land and property were concerned but she did not have to be so in matrimony. Last night she almost cried out her love for Richard when he had taken her to the height of pleasure. But somehow in daylight it had not been appropriate to speak of feelings for each other.

He had made love to her and she hoped he would do so again, so she had to be content for the time being.

They waited until they were called into the court which turned out to be little more than a large office.

At two o'clock their carriage was ready to leave but the second carriage with Brown and the colonel's valet, although loaded, wasn't ready to set off homeward.

"I'm sorry, my dear," Richard said, "one of the horses has cast a shoe and we shall be delayed."

"Oh dear, can't a fresh horse be found?"

"I've just asked them to change the team. I

suggest you remain in the carriage whilst I endeavour to hurry the ostler along."

Richard strode across the yard and noticed three men gathered in one corner. He wouldn't have given them another glance except they appeared out of place dressed in the old style tri-cornered hats and heavy boat cloaks. He tried to hear what they were discussing but he was too far away.

"Colonel Weston, sir," the ostler called, "we have found another team. They are not our finest and might slow your journey but reliable beasts."

"Most obliged to you," Richard said and flipped the man a coin. The fresh team were brought out, the driver, groom and the armed guard climbed aboard and they were off.

When Richard settled into his seat in the carriage, he thought Caroline was looking out of sorts. "Are you unwell, my dear?" he asked.

Her face brightened as she looked at him. "Not in the slightest, now we are on our way. Shall we make Weston Grange before nightfall?"

"I am convinced of it, but are you sure you wish to go there?" He had wanted to ask her before they had arrived in Lichfield but had refrained from doing so. He needed to know if she would be happy living with him, or did she wish to remain at Moreton?

"That is our home, is it not?"

She gave him a sideways glance which ignited a spark of hope in his heart.

"Indeed but I thought you may wish to take possession of Moreton Arnscote."

He watched her tilt her head to one side as if

considering the question and choosing her words carefully before she spoke.

"I thought your mother might wish to remain there. If so I have no objection as I do not see the benefit of an establishment having two mistresses. Such a situation might prove grounds for battle, or at the very least a skirmish or two."

He laughed and took her hand in his. "Mrs. Weston, your intuition does you proud for I could not have put the matter better myself. Indeed, my mother would cling to Moreton at all costs, although I doubt if even she could have remained if Sir Sydney had managed to establish himself there. If that had been her situation then undoubtedly she would have removed to Weston. However, your direction on this matter gives me the greatest of pleasure to see you at Weston and my mother at Moreton."

"It is agreed then?" Caroline smiled and he squeezed her hand. He sank back into the seat content for the first time since Waterloo. His step-father's estate would remain in Moreton hands and perhaps if there were a son born to them, although he would be a Weston, he would have no objection to the boy carrying the Moreton name too. The thought of a son brought him an inner quietness that in time might assuage the guilt he carried about Charles. Lulled by the gentle sway of the carriage, he let his eyelids close and thought of her soft gentle body he had so lovingly caressed the previous night. Marriage? He had no regrets in his choice of bride, even though their wedding had had a somewhat unusual start. Thus occupied in self-appraisement he did not hear the pounding of horsemen approaching until they were almost at passing distance and expected them to race by.

The last thing he expected was the crack of a pistol shot and the cry of highwaymen, "Stand to!"

"By all the saints!" he cried as they were both thrown forwards to the opposite seat. He grabbed Caroline. "Are you injured?"

She shook her head, "Only startled. What is going on?"

As the carriage slowed to a halt, he leant out of the window. Four masked men brandishing pistols were bearing down on them and he could see the armed guard he had employed lying motionless behind in the road. There was no sign of the other carriage.

He dived back to the floor and dragged her down alongside him. "Highwaymen, heavily armed!" He reached under the seat and drew out a wooden box. He flipped open the lid and began loading a pair of duelling pistols. "Do you know how to fire one of these?"

"Yes, my father taught me," she replied in a distraught voice.

"If one of those ruffians tries to violate you, shoot him, aim for his chest and don't forget to cock the pistol." He pressed the weapon into her hand, turned and pulled out a similar box and loaded the other two pistols. Turning to her he said, "Remember you only have one shot, but the handle makes a good club." He saw the colour drain from her face and wanted only to reassure her, but what could he say?

"What do they want? Surely only our money, not our lives," she cried.

"I fear the worst. These men were hanging around the George before we left and who else did we see yesterday?"

"Sir Sydney, but surely he means us no harm now he has the title."

"Don't be naive, he wants the estate too and you are the only person standing in his way."

Another shot rang out, followed by a loud cry as the coachman fell from his seat to the ground. Richard leapt to the window and aimed his pistol at the man who had fired the shot. He didn't wait to see if his shot was successful but dived back to the floor. "Stay down, at all costs, for I am certain you are their quarry."

"Get out of the carriage," an accented voice shouted from outside, "and we will spare you."

Quickly Richard reloaded the pistol. "Did you hear his voice? I'll be dammed if they're not hired French thugs."

"But this is the main road won't there be other carriages or carts along?" Her voice was growing more desperate with every word. "Where's Brown and the baggage?"

"They'll have blocked the road both ways. We're on our own. Listen! We will draw their fire by opening both carriage doors. They will not know from which we intend to descend. I will alight first. Pray that my aim is good."

"Richard you cannot...it could be suicide...I love you. I don't want to lose you!"

He felt his heart squeeze but knew what he had to do, otherwise they could both be murdered in the carriage. "Surprise is our only weapon, believe me."

"I do," she said her voice quivering.

"I will release the doors, when I give the word kick open the other door and remain on the floor. Can you do that?"

"Yes...but,"

"No buts. On the count of three. One, two, three!"

Armed with a pistol in each hand Richard kicked open the door and jumped out, shooting first to his right then to his left. Both shots again found their targets and two other shots rang out from the other side of the carriage. Swiftly he turned, stepped back up and threw his discharged pistols onto the seat. Caroline was sprawled face up on the floor.

He thought she had been shot and lifted her head cradling it in his hands. "Caro! My darling, my love!"

"I shot him." Her eyes stared at him from her chalk white face. "He came to the door with his pistol and I shot him...whatever shall I do? I've...I've killed a man."

He knelt beside her and lifted her onto his lap. "Are you hurt?" he asked, cupped her chin gently with one hand and searched her slender frame for any trace of a wound.

She blinked back at him, "I don't think so...but I've killed a man."

"Hush, my darling, we had to defend ourselves." He wanted to say more, to reassure her, to comfort and hold her close but the sound of another carriage rattling along the road took his attention. "Someone's coming," he whispered. The carriage stopped and Brown and the colonel's valet jumped out.

"Attend to your mistress," Richard ordered and gently lifted Caroline onto the carriage seat. Once he was sure his wife was in the hands of her maid, he jumped down and with the second coachman's assistance went to examine the bodies of the highwaymen lying on the road. They were the men he had seen earlier at the George. Skirting the other side of the carriage, he went down on one knee to inspect the body lying alongside, the man who had shot at Caroline and whom she had shot. Blood oozed from the large wound in the centre of his torso. He knew from his military experience such a wound was fatal. The man would have been dead before he hit the ground.

Richard went down on one knee at the man's side. Light brown eyes stared motionless back at him. They were strangely familiar like the corpse's square portly body. He swallowed deeply as battlefield memories flashed before him. The cold stare of a dead man whose body was still warm proved a haunting vision and silently he prayed this would be the last time he would have to confront death so violently. He eased the kerchief from the man's face and took a deep gasp. He had revealed the body of Sydney Moreton.

CHAPTER TEN

Caroline woke from an uneasy sleep in a strange room. She pushed herself up on her elbows and glanced around. Brown was sitting at the window looking out.

"Where am I?"

The maid turned, stood up and approached the large four-poster bed. "We're in the Talbot Inn in Rugeley," she said. "The Colonel said as it was best we stayed the night here, he having to report to the local magistrate and all."

"Where is he now?" Caroline touched her forehead and realised her head was throbbing. "I don't feel very well."

"The doctor said as you had suffered a great shock and needed a sleeping draught and-"

"Sleeping...have I been given laudanum?"

"Yes, ma'am, I thought as you didn't need it, but the doctor was insistent."

"What's happened? Where's the Colonel? I must speak to him."

"Yes, ma'am, I'll go and see about some tea and ask the landlord to send a message to the Colonel."

When the maid had left the room, Caroline

pulled back the covers and tentatively put her feet to the floor. Slowly she stood up and took a few paces towards the window. She had to make a lunge for the windowsill but she had made it and sank onto the seat below. How weak she felt and what had happened? Then the whole business flooded back, the masked face of the man pointing a pistol at her, his narrow piggy eyes and the flash of a pistol shot. It had been her shot. Convinced she had fired first she felt hollow. Richard's orders were not to hesitate and take advantage of surprise. But what had been the consequences?

She closed her eyes and relived those few blistering seconds. The man had fired but only after she had let loose her pistol at close quarters. She didn't remember seeing him fall as the recoil of the pistol had forced her backwards. Then Richard touched her face, spoke comforting words to her and lifted her onto the seat where Brown wrapped her arms around her. She tried to remember more, but everything went hazy after that.

They must have made their way towards the next town, what did Brown call it? She racked her brain but couldn't remember. Outside in the street below, people went about their daily business, carters driving their wares, servants on their way to the market and delivery boys. The street looked like so many other small market towns, a few shops and half a dozen sheep were being driven down the road by a shepherd in his smock.

Then she saw Richard striding purposely towards a large building at the end of the street. He had his back to her but she knew from the cut of his coat, his broad shoulders and tall upright stance, it could be no other. Her heart leapt, even at a distance his presence was compelling, and how much she loved him.

What had first set her off ? Could she pin-point the moment when her heart reached out to him? Was it when she saw his tall figure standing outside the cottage in Lee Cove? His ruggedness and self-command? Indeed, she thought how his arresting good looks had captured her attention, if not her heart on that day, only she hadn't realised it. But what about now? She had killed a man and the weight of her guilt hung heavily on her slender shoulders.

She stood up and paced the room, unsure of what to do next, terrible thoughts clouded her mind. She folded her arms around her torso and paced some more longing for the safety of either the Weston or Moreton estates. She had worked herself into somewhat of a distressed state when Brown entered carrying a tray.

"Has the Colonel returned yet?"

The maid put the tray down near the bed. "No ma'am, but begging your pardon ma'am, you'd best be back in bed as the Colonel said you were to have rest on account of the terrible events yesterday."

"Yesterday? Yes, of course, what time is it?"

"Why gone noon ma'am. Might be nearer one o'clock by now. Please let me help you. See there's a dish of tea and some warm broth the landlady has made. New baked crusty bread too, ma'am, would you like some?"

Caroline felt her head begin to swim and reached out for Brown's hand. "Help me back to bed."

Sitting up in bed, slowly she let the nourishing soup warm her and picked at small pieces of the bread. She had finished the soup when Richard entered the room a worried expression on his face.

"Leave us and thank the landlady for the soup, it was most welcome."

Brown curtseyed to Richard, collected the tray and quit the room.

Caroline stretched her hand out to him. "Please, come sit, I am worried, my mind is clouded but I know I shot a man and I cannot bring myself to come to terms with what I have done for I am sure the man is dead. Please, Richard, tell me what happened?"

Caroline looked so vulnerable sitting up in bed, her hair tumbling over her shoulders, her eyes wide and appealing that he could not refuse her request, but what could he tell her? That he suspected their attackers had intended to kill them both?

He took a deep breath and hoped she would understand. "My dearest, the men who attacked our carriage were not ordinary highwaymen, if highwaymen can ever be called ordinary. I believe they were hired assassins."

"Hired? By whom?"

"I cannot say. I wounded two but they got away and I doubt they will caught, however there was someone who would have benefited from our demise."

Her hand flew to her mouth as she gasped,

"Sir Sydney!"

"I believe so. It appears his determination to inherit Moreton Arnescote knew no limits."

"But...how? How can he inherit?"

"It is simple, he tried to have our marriage declared null and void when he discovered your existence. Possibly he thought to marry you himself, I do not know what plans he had conjured up but when you had proof that you were indeed the rightful heir to the estate what other course of action could he have taken?"

"I do not understand, how could the estate become his?"

"When a woman marries her property passes to her husband, so Arnscote legally would be mine, however, remove both of us and the property would pass to my nearest relative, possibly my mother as I have no near relations. I suspect Sir Sydney hoped to coerce her into either signing the property over to him or possibly she would meet with an accident and then...both estates would be his."

"Oh, is there no end to his despicable character?"

He noticed how pale her face had become but knew he couldn't keep news from her. "Sydney will no longer trouble us." He clasped her upper arms and drew her towards him.

But she resisted him, pressed her palms on his chest, and created a barrier between them. "He was one of the highway men, wasn't he? And...and I shot him. God forgive me...I have done murder!"

She began to shake and despite her efforts to push him away, he crushed her against his heart, his arms encircling her. She buried her face against his throat as tears rolled down her cheeks and powerful sobs racked her body.

He had no idea how long they remained locked in each other's embrace. However, he knew it was time enough for her sobs to subside and her sensibility to return. At length he lifted her head, marvelling at her loveliness. "We had no choice. You fired your pistol on my command. We acted in self-defence, we are not guilty of murder and no court in the land will convict us, although there will have to be a coroner's court to establish how Sydney died."

"And will I have to give testimony?"

"Not if I can prevent it, however, I have already related the events to the local magistrate and given my surety that we will not leave the county. Arrangements will have to be made for Sydney's funeral." He lifted her chin and gently caressed her lips with his thumb. "Do not worry, my dear, all will be well when we return home."

She had wanted to believe him, but a warning voice had whispered in her head things might never be the same again – *you have killed a man, you have killed your cousin, your kin.* As they journeyed northwards sitting opposite each other in the carriage few words passed between them until they turned off the Stafford road. "I've instructed the driver to take us to Arnscote," Richard said, "Mother will need to be informed and after the shock you have suffered, she is in a better position to look after you than I can at Weston."

Caroline only half-listened as she struggled

with her conscience, but she swallowed hard and tried to comprehend what he was really saying. Did he intend leaving her there? "But...I thought we had agreed on Weston."

"Yes, indeed we did, but circumstances have changed. You need rest and quiet."

"Do you believe I shall get both with your mother? No Richard, I refuse to stay at Arnscote, the estate has brought nothing but trouble into my life even before I had ventured over its threshold."

"And am I to be included in your trouble?"

Awkwardly, she cleared her throat, looked away hastily then turned back to face him. "Last night I said I wanted nothing more than to be your wife and my words were truly spoken but not for just one night, I want to be your wife, live with you at Weston Hall, raise our children there and find happiness and contentment together. How could you ever be included in my troubles when I have come to love and admire you so much? I am troubled because I have killed a relative. Whatever the circumstances I have slain a family member, my kin, my own blood. Although I knew little of the man, his death will stay on my conscience for a long time, but with your support I believe I will learn to live with my feelings and one day forgive myself."

He moved swiftly across the carriage to sit next to her, pulled her roughly into his arms and claimed her lips crushing her against him. His kiss sent shivers of desire racing through her veins as his tongue explored the softness of her mouth and demanded a response.

She couldn't deny him as spirals of ecstasy

raged through her and kissed him back with renewed passion.

When he raised his mouth from hers he gazed hungrily into her eyes. "My dearest Caroline, I love you. Let me protect and comfort you for I know the anguish of feeling responsible for the death of a close relative. The guilt lies inside you and returns to haunt your thoughts when you least expect it."

"Oh, Richard, my pain is small compared with the death of Charles and I had no wish to remind you. Please forgive me. Sir Sydney tried to kill both of us and I must remind myself in my lowest moment that I acted in self-defence."

A wistful smile crossed his lips, "I always tried to convince myself the lives of the men I took in battle were in self-defence too, and for many years I found some succour but when Charles fell it was as if I had fired the cannon." He looked directly into her eyes, "I have been unable to explain my feelings to anyone before. I couldn't trust a soul until now I have you. I love you Caroline Weston and want nothing more than to be your devoted and loving husband. I hope we can raise children and find happiness and peace together."

She wrapped her arms tightly around his neck. "I love you too, Colonel Richard Weston, I love you." Joy burst inside her as she felt his strong protective body next to her. "Take me to bed, husband," she cried.

"What a wanton wench I have married," he replied and unwrapping himself from her embrace lent out of the carriage window. "Change of plan, take us to Weston Grange post haste!"

"What about your mother? Won't she be

anxious for news?"

He turned back to face her. "I swear, not now or ever will Mother come between us. She can wait, can't she?"

Caroline could not reply because his lips had claimed hers once more in a toe-curling, passionate and rewarding kiss to which she abandoned herself to bask in a whirl of happiness and sensation.

The End

If you enjoyed this book you might like other books
by Lynda Dunwell

MARRYING THE ADMIRAL'S DAUGHTER
Sweet Regency Romance

It is 1802 and England is at peace with France., when one of the Royal Navy's most successful frigate captains, Ross Quentin, meets admiral's daughter Bella Richmond, they should be a perfect match. But when did the course of true love ever run smoothly?

Reader's Reviews: *"Excellent reading for the historical/romantic novel fan, with a good plot and very well written. It seamlessly takes the reader back to another time."*

"I love Regencies but there are so few novels that venture to sea with a hero to die for…how I envied Bella Richmond."

Available in Paperback or ebook format from Amazon.

CAPTAIN WESTWOOD'S INHERITANCE
Sweet Regency Romance

A sequel to Marrying the Admiral's Daughter and set in the same Hampshire village. Home from the sea after six years absence, Captain Sir Jonathan Westwood receives news of his father's violent death and discovers his family fortune decimated through treachery. Until he has recovered his family estates he declares he is in no position to offer any lady marriage, even the pretty Miss Ellis.

Talented artist Catherine Ellis is staying in the neighbourhood recovering from a fortunate escape from an unsuitable elopement. She wants to become an artist, but her mill-owner father will not allow it. She falls in love with the dashing Sir Jonathan but believes she is unworthy of him.

With the help of friends, Sir Jonathan struggles against skullduggery and attempted murder to restore the Westwood fortune. He has almost succeeded when Catherine is abducted by pirates bound for France.

Can he save the woman he loves and find happiness?

Available in Paperback or ebook format from Amazon.

ABOUT THE AUTHOR

Lynda Dunwell is a LSE graduate and has taught economics and business studies for twenty years. She has worked as a press officer, advertisement copy writer and tourist information officer.

As a teenager she read the novels of Jane Austen and Georgette Heyer. Today, she still dips into them to rekindle the flavour of Regency life which she adores including, clothes, games, houses, pastimes and even food!

Although based in the landlocked English Midlands, Lynda loves the sea and spends most of her vacations on cruise ships.

She is a member of the UK Romantic Novelists' Association, the Historical Novel Society and the Jane Austen Society.

Another interest is family history. Lynda is a member of the Society of Genealogists, and has traced her paternal family line – the Dunwells – back to 1485. Currently she is researching her female line which she describes as far more challenging.

Website: www.lyndadunwell.com

Or find her on facebook: LyndaDunwell and twitter @LyndaDunwell

19859718R00102

Printed in Great Britain
by Amazon